crash

ALSO BY
LISA McMANN

Wake

Fade

Gone

Cryer's Cross

Dead to You

FOR YOUNGER READERS

The Unwanteds

Island of Silence

Island of Fire

crash

VISIONS BOOK ONE

LISA McMANN

SIMON PULSE

NEW YORK   LONDON   TORONTO   SYDNEY   NEW DELHI

SIMON PULSE
An imprint of Simon & Schuster Children's Publishing Division
1230 Avenue of the Americas, New York, NY 10020
First Simon Pulse hardcover edition January 2013
Copyright © 2013 by Lisa McMann
All rights reserved, including the right of reproduction in whole or in part in any form.
SIMON PULSE and colophon are registered trademarks of Simon & Schuster, Inc.
For information about special discounts for bulk purchases, please contact
Simon & Schuster Special Sales at 1-866-506-1949 or business@simonandschuster.com.
The Simon & Schuster Speakers Bureau can bring authors to your live event.
For more information or to book an event contact the Simon & Schuster Speakers Bureau
at 1-866-248-3049 or visit our website at www.simonspeakers.com.
Designed by Mike Rosamilia
The text of this book was set in Janson Text.
Manufactured in the United States of America
2 4 6 8 10 9 7 5 3 1
Library of Congress Cataloging-in-Publication Data
McMann, Lisa.
Crash / Lisa McMann.
p. cm.
Summary: Sixteen-year-old Jules, whose family owns an Italian restaurant
and has a history of mental illness, starts seeing a recurring vision involving
a rival restaurant, a truck crash, and forbidden love.
ISBN 978-1-4424-0391-8
ISBN 978-1-4424-0592-9 (eBook)
[1. Visions—Fiction. 2. Supernatural—Fiction. 3. Love—Fiction.
4. Families—Fiction. 5. Restaurants—Fiction.] I. Title.
PZ7.M478757Cp 2013
[Fic]—dc23
2012002733

One

My sophomore psych teacher, Mr. Polselli, says knowledge is crucial to understanding the workings of the human brain, but I swear to dog, I don't want any more knowledge about this.

Every few days I see it. Sometimes it's just a picture, like on that billboard we pass on the way to school. And other times it's moving, like on a screen. A careening truck hits a building and explodes. Then nine body bags in the snow.

It's like a movie trailer with no sound, no credits. And nobody sees it but me.

Some days after psych class I hang around by the door of Mr. Polselli's room for a minute, thinking that if I have a mental illness, he's the one who'll be able to tell me. But every time I almost mention it, it sounds too weird to say. *So, uh, Mr. Polselli, when other people see the "turn off your cell phones" screen in the movie theater, I see an extra five-second movie trailer. Er . . . and did I mention I see stills of it on the billboard by my house? You see Jose Cuervo, I see a truck hitting a building and everything exploding. Is that normal?*

The first time was in the theater on the one holiday that our parents don't make us work—Christmas Day. I poked my younger sister, Rowan. "Did you see that?"

She did this eyebrow thing that basically says she thinks I'm an idiot. "See what?"

"The explosion," I said softly.

"You're on drugs." Rowan turned to our older brother, Trey, and said, "Jules is on drugs."

Trey leaned over Rowan to look at me. "Don't do drugs," he said seriously. "Our family has enough problems."

I rolled my eyes and sat back in my seat as the real movie trailers started. "No kidding," I muttered. And I reasoned with myself. The day before I'd almost been robbed while doing a pizza delivery. Maybe I was still traumatized.

I just wanted to forget about it all.

But then on MLK Day this stupid vision thing decided to get personal.

Two

Five reasons why I, Jules Demarco, am shunned:
1. I smell like pizza
2. My parents make us drive a meatball-topped food truck to school for advertising
3. I haven't invited a friend over since second grade
4. Did I mention I smell like pizza? Like, its umami*-ness oozes from my pores
5. Everybody at school likes Sawyer Angotti's family's restaurant better

Frankly, I don't blame them. I'd shun me too.

---

*look it up

Every January my mother says Martin Luther King Jr. weekend gives us the boost we need to pay the rent after the first two dead weeks of the year. She's superpositive about everything. It's like she forgets that every month is the same. Her attitude is probably what keeps our business alive. But if my mother, Paula, is the backbone of Demarco's Pizzeria, my father, Antonio, is the broken leg that keeps us struggling to catch up.

There's no school on MLK Day, so Trey and I are manning the meatball truck in downtown Chicago, and Rowan is working front of house in the restaurant for the lunch shift. She's jealous. But Trey and I are the oldest, so we get to decide.

The food truck is actually kind of a blast, even if it does have two giant balls on top, with endless jokes to be made. Trey and I have been cooking together since we were little—he's only sixteen months older than me. He's a senior. He's supposed to be the one driving the food truck to school because he has his truck license now, but he pays me ten bucks a week to secretly drive it so he can bum a ride from our neighbor Carter. Carter is kind of a douche, but at least his piece-of-crap Buick doesn't have a sack on its roof.

Trey drives now and we pass the billboard again.

"Hey—what was on the billboard?" I ask as nonchalantly as I can.

Trey narrows his eyes and glances at me. "Same as always. Jose Cuervo. Why?"

"Oh." I shrug like it's no big deal. "Out of the corner of my eye I thought it had changed to something new for once." Weak answer, but he accepts it. To me, the billboard is a still picture of the explosion. I look away and rub my temples as if it will make me see what everybody else sees, but it does nothing. Instead, I try to forget by focusing on my phone. I start posting all over the Internet where Demarco's Food Truck is going to be today. I'm sure some of our regulars will show up. It's becoming a sport, like storm chasing. Only they're giant meatball chasing.

Some people need a life. Including me.

We roll past Angotti's Trattoria on the way into the city—that's Sawyer's family's restaurant. Sawyer is working today too. He's outside sweeping the snow from their sidewalk. I beg for the traffic light to stay green so we can breeze past unnoticed, but it turns yellow and Trey slows the vehicle. "You could've made it," I mutter.

Trey looks at me while we sit. "What's your rush?"

I glance out the window at Sawyer, who either hasn't noticed our obnoxious food truck or is choosing to ignore it.

Trey follows my glance. "Oh," he says. "The enemy. Let's wave!"

I shrink down and pull my hat halfway over my eyes.

"Just . . . hurry," I say, even though there's nothing Trey can do. Sawyer turns around to pick up a bag of rock salt for the ice, and I can tell he catches sight of our truck. His head turns slightly so he can spy on who's driving, and then he frowns.

Trey nods coolly at Sawyer when their eyes meet, and then he faces forward as the light finally changes to green. "Do you still like him?" he asks.

Here's me, sunk down in the seat like a total loser, trying to hide, breathing a sigh of relief when we start rolling again. "Yeah," I say, totally miserable. "Do you?"

Three

Trey smiles. "Nah. That urban underground thing he's got going on is nice, and of course I'm fond of the, ah, Mediterranean complexion, but I've been over him for a while. He's too young for me. You can have him."

I laugh. "Yeah, right. Dad will love that. Maybe me hooking up with an Angotti will be the thing that puts him over the edge." I don't mention that Sawyer won't even look at me these days, so the chance of me "having" Sawyer is zero.

Sawyer Angotti is not the kind of guy most people would say is hot, but Trey and I have the same taste in men, which is sometimes convenient and sometimes a pain in the ass. Sawyer has this street casual look where he could totally be a clothes model, but if he ever told people he was one, they'd be like, "Seriously? No way." Because his most attractive features are so subtle, you know? At first glance he's really ordinary, but if you study him . . . big sigh. His vulnerable smile is what gets me—not the charming one he uses on teachers and girls and probably customers, too. I mean the warm, crooked smile that doesn't come out unless he's feeling shy or self-conscious. That one makes my stomach flip. Because for the most part, he's tough-guy metro, if such a thing exists. Arms crossed and eyebrow raised, constantly questioning the world. But I've seen his other side a million times. I've been in love with him since we played plastic cheetahs and bears together at indoor recess in first grade.

How was I supposed to know back then that Sawyer was the enemy? I didn't even know his last name. And I didn't know about the family rivalry. But the way my father interrogated me after they went to my first parent-teacher conference and found out that I "played well with others" and "had a nice friend in Sawyer Angotti," you'd have thought I'd given away great-grandfather's last weapon to the enemy. Trey says that was right around the time Dad really started acting weird.

All I knew was that I wasn't allowed to play cheetahs and bears with Sawyer anymore. I wasn't even supposed to talk to him.

But I still did, and he still did, and we would meet

under the slide and trade suckers from the candy jar each of our restaurants had by the cash register. I would bring him grape, and he always brought me butterscotch, which we never had in our restaurant. I'd do anything to get Sawyer Angotti to give me a butterscotch sucker again.

I have a notebook from sixth grade that has nine pages filled with embarrassing and overdramatic phrases like "I pine for Sawyer Angotti" and "JuleSawyer forever." I even made an *S* logo for our conjoined names in that one. Too bad it looks more like a cross between a dollar sign and an ampersand. I'd dream about us getting secretly married and never telling our parents.

And back then I'd moon around in my room after Rowan was asleep, pretending my pillow was Sawyer. Me and my Sawyer pillow would lie down on my bed, facing one another, and I'd imagine us in Bulger Park on a blanket, ignoring the tree frogs and pigeons and little crying kids. I'd touch his cheek and push his hair back, and he'd look at me with his gorgeous green eyes and that crooked, shy grin of his, and then he'd lean toward me and we'd both hold our breath without realizing it, and his lips would touch mine, and then . . . He'd be my first kiss, which I'd never forget. And no matter how much our parents tried to keep us apart, he'd never break my heart.

Oh, sigh.

But then, on the day before seventh grade started,

when it was time to visit school to check out classes and get our books, his father was there with him, and my father was there with me, and I did something terrible.

Without thinking, I smiled and waved at my friend, and he smiled back, and I bit my lip because of love and delight after not seeing him for the whole summer . . . and his father saw me. He frowned, looked up at my father, scowled, and then grabbed Sawyer's arm and pulled him away, giving my father one last heated glance. My father grumbled all the way home, issuing half-sentence threats under his breath.

And that was the end of that.

I don't know what his father said or did to him that day, but by the next day, Sawyer Angotti was no longer my friend. Whoever said seventh grade is the worst year of your life was right. Sawyer turned our friendship off like a faucet, but I can't help it—my faucet of love has a really bad leak.

Trey parks the truck as close to the Field Museum as our permit allows, figuring since the weather is actually sunny and not too freezing and windy, people might prefer to grab a quick meal from a food truck instead of eating the overpriced generic stuff inside the tourist trap.

Before we open the window for business, we set up. Trey checks the meat sauce while I grate fresh mozzarella into tiny, easily meltable nubs. It's a simple operation—our winter truck specialty is an Italian bread bowl with spicy mini meatballs, sauce, and cheese. The truth is it's delicious, even though I'm sick to death of them.

We also serve our pizza by the slice, and we're talking deep-dish Chicago-style, not that thin crap that Angotti's serves. Authentic, authschmentic. The tourists want the hearty, crusty, saucy stuff with slices of sausage the diameter of my bicep and bubbling cheese that stretches the length of your forearm. That's what we've got, and it's amazing.

Oh, but the Angotti's sauce . . . I had it once, even though in our house it's contraband. Their sauce will lay you flat, seriously. It's that good. We even have the recipe, apparently, but we can't use it because it's patented and they sell it by the jar—it's in all the local stores and some regional ones now too. My dad about had an aneurysm when that happened. Because, according to Dad, in one of his mumble-grumble fits, the Angottis had been after our recipe for generations and somehow managed to steal it from us.

So I guess that's how the whole rivalry started. From what I understand, and from what I know about Sawyer avoiding me like the plague, his parents feel the same way about us as my parents feel about them.

Trey and I pull off a really decent day of sales for the middle of January. We hightail it back home for the dinner rush so we can help Rowan out.

As we get close, we pass the billboard from the other side. I locate it in my side mirror, and it's the same as this morning. Explosion. I watch it grow small and disappear, and then close my eyes, wondering what the hell is wrong with me.

We pull into the alley and park the truck, take the stuff inside.

"Get your asses out there!" Rowan hisses as she flies through the kitchen. She gets a little anxious when people have to wait ten seconds. That kid is extremely well put together, but she carries the responsibility of practically the whole country on her shoulders.

Mom is rolling out dough. I give her a kiss on the cheek and shake the bank bag in her face to show her I'm on the way to putting it in the safe like I'm supposed to. "Pretty good day. Had a busload of twenty-four," I say.

"Fabulous!" Mom says, way too perky. She grabs a tasting utensil, reaches into a nearby pot, and forks a meatball for me. I let her shove it into my mouth when I pass her again.

"I's goo'!" I say. And really freaking hot. It burns the roof of my mouth before I can shift it between my teeth to let it cool.

Tony, the cook who has been working for our family restaurant for something like forty million years, smiles at me. "Nice work today, Julia," he says. Tony is one of the few people I allow to call me by my birth name.

I guess my dad, Antonio, was actually named after Tony. Tony and my grandfather came to America together. I don't really remember my grandpa much—he killed himself when I was little. Depression. A couple of years ago I accidentally found out it was suicide when I overheard Mom and Aunt Mary talking about it.

When I asked my mom about it later, she didn't deny it—instead, she said, "But you kids don't have any sign of depression in you, so don't worry. You're all fine." Which was about the best way to make me think I'm doomed.

It's a weird thing to find out about your family, you know? It made me feel really different for the rest of the day, and it still does now whenever I think about it. Like we're all wondering where the depression poison will hit next, and we're all looking at my dad. I wonder if that's why my mother is so upbeat all the time. Maybe she thinks she can protect us with her happy shield.

Trey and I hurry to wash up, grab fresh aprons, and check in with Aunt Mary at the hostess stand. She's seating somebody, so we take a look at the chart and see that the house is pretty full. No wonder Rowan's freaking out.

Rowan's fifteen and a freshman. Just as Trey is sixteen months older than me, she's sixteen months younger. I don't know if my parents planned it, and I don't want to know, but there it is. I pretty much think they had us for the sole purpose of working for the family business. We started washing dishes and busing tables years ago. I'm not sure if it was legal, but it was definitely tradition.

Rowan looks relieved to see us. She's got the place under control, as usual. "Hey, baby! Go take a break," I whisper to her in passing.

"Nah, I'm good. I'll finish out my tables," she says. I glance at the clock. Technically, Rowan is supposed to quit at seven, because she's not sixteen yet—she can only work late in the summer—but, well, tradition trumps rules sometimes. Not that my parents are slave drivers or anything. They're not. This is just their life, and it's all they know.

It's a busy night because of the holiday. Busy is good. Busy means we can pay the rent, and whatever else comes up. Something always does.

By ten thirty all the customers have left. Even though Dad hasn't come down at all this evening to help out, Mom says she and Tony can handle closing up alone, and she sends Trey and me upstairs to the apartment to get some sleep.

I don't want to go up there.

Neither does Trey.

Four

Trey and I go out the back and into the door to the stairs leading up to our home above the restaurant. We pick our way up the stairs, through the narrow aisle that isn't piled with stuff. At the top, we push against the door and squeeze through the space.

Rowan has already done what she could with the kitchen. The sink is empty, the counters are clean. The kitchen is the one sacred spot, the one room where Mom won't take any garbage from anybody—literally. Because even after cooking all day, she still likes to be able to cook at home too, without having to worry that Dad's precious stacks of papers are going to combust and set the whole building on fire because they're too close to the gas stove.

Everywhere else—dining room, living room, and

hallway—is piled high around the edges with Dad's stuff. Lots of papers—recipes and hundreds of cooking magazines, mostly, and all the Chicago newspapers from the past decade. Shoe boxes, shirt boxes, and every other possible kind of box you can imagine, some filled with papers, some empty. Plastic milk crates filled with cookbooks and science books and gastronomy magazines. Bags full of greeting cards, birthday cards, sympathy cards, some written in, some brand-new, meant for good intentions that never happened. Hundreds of old videos, and a stack as high as my collarbone of old VCRs that don't work. Stereos, 8-track players, record players, tape recorders, all broken. Records and cassette tapes and CDs and games— oh my dog, the board games. Monopoly, Life, Password, Catch Phrase. Sometimes five or six duplicates, most of them with little yellowing masking-tape stickers on them that say seventy-five cents or a buck twenty-five. Insanity. Especially when somebody puts something heavy on top of a Catch Phrase and that stupid beeper goes off somewhere far below, all muffled.

We weave through it. Thankfully, Dad is nowhere to be found, either asleep or buried alive under all his crap. It's not like he's violent or mean or anything. He's just . . . unpredictable. When he's feeling good, he's in the restaurant. He's visible. He's easy to keep track of. But on the days he doesn't come down, we never know what to expect.

We climb those stairs after the end of our shift knowing he could be standing right there in the kitchen, long-faced, unshaven, having surfaced to eat something for the first time since yesterday. And rattling off the same guilt-inspired apologies, day after day after day. *I just couldn't make it down today. Not feeling up to it. I'm sorry you kids have to work so hard.* What do you say to that after the tenth time, or the hundredth?

Worse, he could be sitting in the dark living room with his hands covering his face, the blue glow from the muted TV spotlighting his depressed existence so we can't ignore it. It's probably wrong that Trey and Rowan and I all hope he stays invisible, holed up in his bedroom on days like these, but it's just easier when he's out of sight. We can pretend depressed Dad doesn't exist.

Tonight we breathe a sigh of relief. Trey heads into the cluttered bathroom, its cupboards overflowing with enough soap, shampoo, toothpaste, and toilet paper to get us through Y3K. Thank God our bedrooms are off-limits to Dad. I peek into my tidy little room and see Rowan is sleeping in her bed already, but I'm still wired from a long day. I close the door quietly and grab a glass of milk from the kitchen, then settle down in the one chair in the living room that's not full of stuff and flip on the TV. I run through the DVR list, choosing a rerun of an old Sherlock Holmes movie that I've been watching a little bit at a time over the past couple of weeks, whenever I get a chance. Somebody else must be watching it too, because it's not cued up to the last part I watched. I hit the slowest fast-forward so I can find where I left off.

Trey peeks his head in the room. "Night," he says. He dangles the keys to the meatball truck, and when I hold out my hand, he tosses them to me.

"Thanks," I say, not meaning it. I shouldn't have agreed to only ten bucks a week, but I was desperate. It's not nearly enough to pay for the humiliation of driving the giant balls. "Where's my ten bucks?"

"Isn't it only eight if one day is a holiday?" He gives me what he thinks is his adorable face and hands me a five and three ones.

"Sorry. Not in the contract." I hold my hand out for more.

"Dammit." He goes back to his room for two more dollars while Sir Henry on the TV is flitting around outside on the moors in fast mode, which looks kind of kooky.

Trey returns. "Here."

I grab the two bucks from him and shove all ten into my pocket with my tips. "Thanks. Night."

When he's gone, I stop the fast-forward, knowing I went too far, and rewind to the commercial as I slip the keys into my other pocket, then press play.

Instead of the movie that I'm expecting, I see *it* again.

It flashes by in a few seconds, and then it's gone. The truck, the building, the explosion. And then back to our regularly scheduled programming.

"Stop it," I whisper. My stomach flips and a creepy shiver runs down my neck. It makes my throat tighten. I pause the recording and sit there a minute, trying to calm down. And then I hit rewind.

Ninety-nine percent of me hopes there's nothing there but a creepy giant hound on the moor.

But there it is.

I watch it again, and I get this gnawing thing in my chest, like I'm supposed to do something about it.

"Why does this keep happening?" I mutter, and rewind it again. I hit play and it all flies by so fast, I can hardly see it. I rewind once more and this time set it to play in slow motion.

The truck is yellow. I notice it's actually a snowplow, and the snow is falling pretty hard. It's dark outside, but the streetlamps are lit. The truck is coming fast and it starts angling slightly, crossing to the wrong side and going off the road. It jumps the curb spastically and jounces over some snow piles in a big parking lot, and then I see the building—there's a large window—for a split second before the truck hits it. The building explodes shortly after contact, glass and brick shrapnel flying everywhere. The scene cuts to the body bags in the snow. I count again to make sure—definitely nine. The last frame is a close-up of three of the bags, and then it's over. I hit the pause button.

"What are you doing?"

I jump and whirl around to see Rowan standing in the doorway squinting at me, hair all disheveled. "Jeez!" I whisper, trying to calm my heartbeat. "You scared the crap out of me." I glance back at the TV with slow-motion dread, like I've just been caught looking at . . . I don't know. Porn, or something else I'm not supposed to look at. But it's paused at a sour cream commercial. I let out a breath of relief and turn my attention back to Rowan.

She shrugs. "Sorry. I thought I heard Mom come up."

"Not yet. Not for a while."

She scratches her head, the sleeve of her boy jammies wagging against her cheek. "You coming to bed soon? Or do you want me to stay up with you?"

Her sweet, sleepy disposition is one of my favorites, maybe because she can be so mellow and generous when she just wakes up. I suck in my bottom lip, thinking, and look at the remote control in my hand. "Nah, I'm coming to bed now. Just gotta brush my teeth."

She scrunches up her face and yawns. "What time is it?"

I laugh softly. "Around eleven, I guess. Eleven fifteen."

"Okay," she says, turning to go back down the hallway to our bedroom. "Night."

I look at the TV once more and close my weary eyes for a moment. Then I turn it off and stand up, setting the remote on top of the set so it doesn't get buried, and carefully pick my way to the bathroom, and on to bed. But I don't think I'll be sleeping anytime soon.

Five

Five minutes later and Rowan's breathing sounds like she's asleep again. I wish I could just drift off like that. Instead, I lie here watching the wall opposite the window, where faint pulsing light from our restaurant sign beats out a song nobody knows or hears.

The movie theater. The billboard. Now TV commercials. What could be next? Ten minutes crawl by. Fifteen. And I may as well get up and get it over with.

I slip back out to the living room and cue it all up again, staring at the TV like I'm in some kind of weird hypnotic zone, not seeing the movie at all. I rub my bleary eyes and hit slow play, and it's there like before. A few seconds later there's the close-up of the three body bags, and then it's over and the commercial starts.

I rewind to see if I can pause the scene on the body bags close-up, which I hadn't really noticed before in the regular-speed version. It's like a hidden frame at regular speed, too fast for the human brain to comprehend.

I hit the slow-play button and then wait for it, and pause it at the exact right moment. It's a slightly blurry shot, but it's obvious what I'm looking at. I scan the picture, noting that one of the bags isn't zipped up all the way. The plastic is folded over at the top corner, and the head of the dead body is exposed. I'm strangely drawn to it out of curiosity, rather than repulsed by it.

I squint for a better look. And then my heart bangs around in my chest and I lean forward, get down on the cluttered floor, and crawl to the TV to get a better look.

And then I suck in a scream.

The dead face belongs to Sawyer Angotti.

I scramble to my feet and stumble back to the chair, grab the remote, and hit the power button so many times I actually turn the thing off, then on, then off again before my brain can compute that I've gotten rid of the image from the TV.

My heart won't stop freaking out inside my chest. "No way," I whisper, as if that will take away the scene I just saw. "No way, no way, no way."

I pinch my arm to make sure I'm not having a nightmare, and it hurts, so I think this is real. I pace in the narrow carpeted space that isn't covered by hoards of junk, talking to myself, trying to calm down. But I can't.

Why am I seeing this?

What the hell is going on?

I go back to the remote and turn the TV on, flinching and shuddering as I delete the movie. Then I delete a bunch of other stuff that Rowan will kill me for, but I can't help it. I need to get these images away from me. I need to get this scene off my TV, off my billboard, out of my local theater, and make it go away.

When I hit the power button again, I'm enveloped in darkness, and I can't stop thinking about dead bodies lying in wait under Dad's piles of junk. It's like a nightmare, only I'm not asleep, my mind playing tricks on me. I skitter to my room and get into bed where it's safe, pulling my blankets up to my chin and hugging my pillow. My Sawyer pillow.

I toss and turn, checking the clock every few minutes. Willing my mind to go blank, willing myself to go to sleep, which makes it even more impossible. I have this ridiculous urge to call Sawyer to make sure he's alive, but tell myself I'll be mortified at school tomorrow if I do that. I mean, I just saw him alive this morning! There's no way he could be dead.

After a while I hear Mom coming up the steps. She

clatters in the kitchen, and then I can hear her moving things around in the living room, probably throwing junk away. A while later she makes her way to her bedroom, where she and Dad will sleep until nine thirty or ten, and then she'll get up and do the restaurant thing all over again, with or without my dad.

Eventually, I calm down. Sometime after two I drift off, the vision following me into my dreams.

Six

Six a.m. comes fast. We three kids all stupidly get up at the same time every morning—hey, old habits are hard to break; besides, we miss each other *so much* after literally hours of being apart. Automatically Rowan and I kick ourselves loose from our blankets and race to the door. I whip it open, and there's Trey emerging from his room. Expertly, and almost quietly, we jostle and shove each other in the packed hallway as we jockey for the first slot in the bathroom. Trey shoves his butt against my hip and throws me off balance, knocking me into Rowan, who almost pitches a whole stack of Christmas cookie tins over—holy shit, what a racket that would be! I swallow a snort and Trey strikes a triumphant Gaga pose in the bathroom doorway before sliding in and closing the door. It's kind of like we live in that *Silent Library* game show and we're all trying to be superquiet while competing to win at a ridiculously noisy challenge, which makes everything so much more hilarious.

But once I have a minute to remember what happened last night, the fun evaporates and I start getting this recurring wave of nausea. I can't handle the thought of breakfast right now, so I pocket a granola bar for later. After an hour, when I'm waiting for Rowan to finish her makeup so we can go, I cautiously flip on the TV, hoping I can find the news and not a creepy encore of last night. Thankfully, there's just some morning talk show. No mention of explosions or body bags. No weird vision taunting me.

Trey slips past me and flies down the stairs two at a time without saying good-bye. We'll see each other at school. We're in the same lunch and sculpting class—which we of course elected to take because why the heck not bring our pizza-crust-making skills to a new level with clay? The other day I was making a plate on the potter's wheel and nearly threw it up into the air when I was daydreaming about Sawyer.

My stomach clenches again.

Sawyer. Body bag. Is he dead already?

In the hallway outside the bathroom, I jiggle the door handle and whisper as harshly as I can, "Hurry up, Rowan!"

Finally she comes.

•   •   •

We ease out of the alley in the meatball truck. Today's trip to school is brought to you by two chicks with big balls. Har har. Rowan flips down the mirrored sun visor and puts on lip gloss, then fusses with her hair. A minute later she sighs and snaps the visor back up, slouching into the seat like she's given up on her looks for the day. She's been fussy about her looks a lot lately. I think she's got a crush, but I don't say anything. She pulls out her phone and takes a picture of herself and then studies it. I smile and focus on the road.

Traffic is busy, making every block agonizingly slow, and I'm hitting almost all the lights red. I tell myself not to look at the billboard as we pass, and almost manage it. But I steal a glance at the last second, and there's no Cuervo . . . just the crash. At school we park in the back of the lot, which is the only place the truck fits.

I sprint through the parking lot to the school, hugging my book bag and avoiding icy spots, leaving Rowan behind. Inside I speed walk to my locker and look down the hall like I always do, to where Sawyer is usually standing, hanging out with his friends, some of whom are my former friends.

I stand on my tiptoes, straining to see through the crowd.

At first I don't see him, but then, thank the dogs, there he is in his usual spot. How weird is it that I feel my eyes well up with tears of relief for a second? He glances my way, and I almost duck, but realize at the last moment that that would look even more stupid than me staring, so I quickly turn my head and stare into my locker, blinking hard.

And then my respiratory system checks in, reminding me to breathe before I pass out. Sweat pricks my scalp. I whip my hat off and slip out of my jacket, and then try to smooth down my flyaway hair in the little mirror I have inside my locker door.

I want to start walking to class, but my legs are still a little too weak to keep me from tripping down the hallway. The whole time I'm standing here, all I can think about is how Sawyer isn't dead. This vision thing scared the living crap out of me for no good reason. These crazy scenes I'm seeing are meaningless. So I guess there's maybe something wrong . . . with me.

All I know is that it can't be a mental illness.

Not like depression. Not like hoarding.

Please . . . it just can't be like those things at all.

Seven

I don't look at the billboard. I don't turn on the TV.
I don't go to any movies. For a week, I keep my head down,
go to school, go to work, do homework, go to bed. Still,
every morning at school I look over at Sawyer to make sure
he's alive.

He always is.

Five reasons why I love a guy who won't talk to me:
1. In first grade he always let me be the cheetah
2. He's kind to people, even the unpopular ones,
    and if I ever really needed him, I bet he'd
    help me
3. He isn't gross
4. He's soft-spoken, under the radar, but

somehow everybody seems to know and
like him

5. He volunteers at the Humane Society on
Saturday mornings

Do I think Sawyer has something against my family?
Sure, he has to. But he's not *mean* to me—he just ignores
me most of the time now. Still, when we were forced to
pair up for a science project in ninth grade, we talked
almost like normal, which gave me so much hope it practically killed me after the project was over and things went
back to the way they were.

I don't get it. I'm just not really into the drama of this
whole family-rivalry thing. It stresses me out. I'm guessing
he's not into it either, because we never talked about it. We
never discussed seventh grade and what happened. Now
I sort of appreciate that about him, because it could have
started a big fight, and we could have ended up having a
major problem. And I know that if classmates began taking
sides, he'd win epically.

Outside of forced projects, we steer clear of one
another, because obviously I'm not going to follow him
around. Much. It's not like I don't have other shit to do
besides moon around after a boy. I mean, I watch him,
though. Like, all the time, but I'm not a creep or anything. And I eavesdrop. That's how I know about him

volunteering at the Humane Society. I really hope one day I'll get over him. Sometimes I think I'm past it all, but then he does that smile and reality hits.

Saturday morning, on our way into the city for the lunch rush, I make Trey drive past the Humane Society to see if Sawyer's car is there. It is. I don't know why I keep worrying about him when ignoring all of this is what I really want to do, but I can't shake that image of his dead face from my mind.

"What's going on with you?" Trey asks after a while.

"Just tired," I say automatically. It's the stock answer in our house whenever we don't want to talk. Everybody understands tired—nobody questions it, nobody tries to talk you out of it.

But Trey knows me better than anybody. "Why don't you ever do anything for fun?"

I snort. "When?"

"Mom will give you nights off for stuff. You know that."

"I . . . don't have anything else to do."

"You could go see a movie—"

"No," I say.

Trey glances at me at a stoplight as we near our destination. I stare straight ahead. I can't look at him or he'll know something's wrong. I focus on the construction crews along the side of the street hanging up banners for a spring flower show at the conservatory. In that instant, all the banners, as far ahead of us as I can see, change.

I suck in a breath. The banners now advertise dead Sawyer Angotti's face.

"What's wrong?" Trey asks. His voice is concerned.

"Nothing," I say. I lean down and pretend to rummage around in my purse. "Seriously. I just need more sleep."

"I don't believe you."

I don't know what to say to that. Besides, it's time to park the balls and feed some hungry people.

Every time I hand food out the window to the customers, I catch the long line of banners out of the corner of my eye and see Sawyer's dead face. "Go away," I mutter.

A customer looks at me, taken aback.

"Oh, no—not you," I say. "I'm so sorry." Great, now I'm insulting customers and talking to the banners. No mental illness here.

I keep my eyes closed for the ride home.

Eight

Back at the restaurant for the dinner rush, Dad is in the kitchen with his chef jacket on, which is a good sign. Trey and I exchange a glance and Trey calls out, "Hey, Pops."

Dad looks up and smiles. "How's my boy?" His voice booms. It always has. He's been startling innocent children for as long as I can remember. Luckily, Trey did not inherit that trait. "Did you have a good day? Where'd you end up? Any other trucks out in this weather?" He can never just ask one question when he's feeling good.

I let Trey handle him and keep walking, grabbing a fresh apron and tying it around my waist on my way to the hostess stand.

"Hey, Aunt Mary," I say. She's my dad's sister. She

reaches for me and air-kisses my cheek, then squeezes my upper arm and shakes me like she's been doing since I was a little girl.

"So beautiful!" she declares loudly. "You have your father's face."

Yeah . . . uh . . . thanks. That's not, like, a weird thing to say to a girl or anything. I smile and ask, "Is it busy? Where's Rowan?"

"Tables seven and eight—a ten-topper. Rowdy bunch of hooligans. Maybe Trey should help her."

I try not to scowl. Aunt Mary still lives in the last century. "I'm sure she and I can handle it fine. Trey's doing deliveries tonight. He's talking to Dad."

Aunt Mary gives me a knowing look.

We never discuss Dad's little "problem" with anybody. It's this huge secret everybody knows but nobody talks about. Nobody's allowed in our apartment. Nobody who knows us personally asks why. Just invoking Dad's name is enough to stop Aunt Mary from pressing the issue. Talk about power. The guy who does the weirdest shit has all the power.

I grab a pen and an order pad, head into the dining room, and catch Rowan's eye. She gives me a stricken look and points with a sideways nod to the big group. I look, and my heart sinks. It's a bunch of kids from school, looking like they're all on one giant, icky date. With a glance I see three guys who have tortured Trey in one manner or another since middle school. Two of the girls, Roxie and Sarah, used to be my friends in elementary school, before the cliques formed. Roxie was even upstairs for my sixth birthday party, back before the formation of the psycho's dump.

I get the status from Rowan and help her bring out the drink orders. I smile politely at anyone who catches my eye. I am not here to socialize. I am here to serve as their nanny and slave, clean up when they make a huge sticky mess of sodden sugar packets, hot-pepper water glasses, and clogged parm shakers, and smile gratefully as I watch them not leave a tip. And I will promptly dismiss it from memory the next time I see them, when they call out in the hallway, "Hey, Jules, how are the big balls treating you?" Because that is what we Demarcos do to survive and pay the bills. And we do it well.

"Oh, hey, Julia," Roxie says. I don't remind her that I've gone by Jules since third grade.

And I do not call her Roxanne in return. "What can I get for you, Roxie? Or do you guys need a few minutes to decide?"

Half of them haven't acknowledged me at all, and the other half give each other that smirky, *Hey, we should probably check out the menu* look, and no one answers my question. I stand a moment more, and then say, "So, you need a few minutes?"

"Yeah," a couple of them say.

"I'll stop back. If you decide before I get here, just flag me down."

Silence.

"Okay, great." I walk away feeling like a big bucket of stupid. My face gets hot. I hear the order-up bell, so I make a beeline for the kitchen to grab food for Rowan.

Trey is headed my way. I put my hand out. "Don't go out there," I say, and that stops him. I give him a sympathetic smile.

"Who's here?"

"Assholes. Don't worry, we've got it covered for now. I'll let you clean up after them."

"Awesome," he says, rolling his eyes, but I know he's grateful. It's not like Trey needs anybody to protect him, but with Dad in the kitchen tonight, none of us want any trouble out on the floor. And with that cast of bigots out there, there would most certainly be trouble. Trey turns around and starts helping Casey, the dishwasher, while I grab the pizza and spaghetti for table four and head back out.

Over at the group-date table, I see straw wrapper carcasses all over the floor. "What sounds good tonight?" I say, perky. I hold my order pad so they get a clue that it's time.

"Angotti's sounds good," one jackass says, "but they're closed."

I look up sharply. "On a Saturday night? Why, did something happen?"

The guy shrugs.

I stare. Why on earth would Angotti's be closed? Angotti's never closes. There has to be a family tragedy for that to happen.

"Um . . . ," Roxie says. "Hello . . ." She waves her menu in my face and I look at her, my stomach twisting. "We'll have two large pepperoni pizzas and a supreme. Thin crust." She hands me her menu.

I picture Sawyer Angotti's dead face staring back at me where my grandfather's face is.

"We don't have thin crust," I say in a weird, wispy voice that doesn't even sound like me. The table wavers. I glance over at Rowan, then back at Roxie. "I have to go," I whisper.

I drop the menu on the table and take off. As I pass Rowan I say, "Can you help them? I think I'm going to be sick," and I just keep going, running now, through the kitchen, out the back door, calling out, "Ma, help out front, please," before the door closes. I suck in a cold breath of air and hang on to the door handle before I go into the apartment stairwell and run up, bumping against stacks of stuff on my way to the living room. I grab the TV remote, turn it on, and pick up the phone, but my hand is shaking and I don't know the number. I can't think.

On TV is a gardening show. I pause and play, and it's still the show.

I drop the remote in the chair and whirl around. "Phone book," I mutter. I look around the room at all the junk, no idea where to start. My chest floods with panic. "Where's the fucking phone book? God! I hate this stupid place!" I start whipping through four-foot piles of magazines looking for a phone book, knowing there are probably no fewer than fifty of them in this room, yet not a single one shows its face. I go to the little desk drawer, and it's jam-packed with paper clips. I can't even slam it shut, it's so full. I pinch my eyelids, trying not to cry in frustration. Just trying to breathe and think.

And then the TV sound goes off, all on its own.

Nine

I look over at the TV screen, and there it is. Only this time it's a longer clip.

The snowplow crosses to the wrong side of the street, careens up over the snow pile and curb of the parking lot, almost getting airborne, and lands, bouncing. Not slowing down. I see the building for a split second, the big long window, and then the crash and the explosion. Bricks and glass go flying.

And then there's a new part: The building catches on fire, and through the dark smoke, I see the structure as if we are fleeing from the scene, and we're panning wide. It's a three-story. A striped awning hangs precariously from a part of the wall that is still intact. And then everything is gone, and I'm watching a commercial for bug spray.

"What do you want me to do about it?" I yell at the TV. "I'm just a kid! Leave me alone!"

I stare at the phone in my hand, and my head clears. I dial 411. "Melrose Park," I say, my voice shaking. "Angotti's Trattoria." A moment later I get the automated number, and push to dial direct.

It rings.

Five times it rings, like bells tolling for the dead.

And then it stops ringing, and a man's voice announces, "Angotti's."

I am stunned and can't speak at first. I clear my throat and realize I don't know what to say. "Um, are you . . . I mean, how late are you open?"

"We're actually closed to the public tonight for a family wedding reception. Really sorry about that. We'll be open again tomorrow, eleven to eleven."

"Oh." I breathe out a relieved sigh into the phone, and then curse myself. "Okay, eleven to eleven. I—I was just checking. Thanks." I want to ask, *Is Sawyer alive?* I want to ask, *Are you sure it's not a death in the family?* But my heart is stuck in my throat.

And then the man says, "Jules?"

Shit. I'm a terrible liar when confronted. "Yeah," I say.

"It's Sawyer."

"Oh. You sounded . . . older."

His voice turns quiet, like he's trying not to let people

hear. "Why the heck are you calling the restaurant?"

"How did you know it was me?"

"Caller ID says 'A. Demarco.' And by your voice."

I answer with another little breathy noise that I think probably sounds like a dog panting. He recognized my voice.

"So why . . . ?" he asks again. "Are you trying to spy or something?" he says, like he's starting to wind up. "If so, you're not very good at it. I can't believe your parents are making you do this."

"No, Sawyer," I say. "That's not why . . ." I can hardly talk. I'm so relieved to hear his voice.

"So, what, you want a reservation?" He laughs sarcastically.

"No," I say in a firmer voice, "and stop accusing me of stupid things. I just heard from a customer that you guys are closed tonight. And—" I grip the top of my head with my free hand, hoping that'll help me think of a lie. "And . . . you guys never close. So, ah, I just wanted to make sure you were okay." Crap. I barely get the words out when I hear footsteps coming up the steps, and I remember the disaster I left Rowan with downstairs.

Sawyer doesn't answer.

"I'm sorry," I whisper. I hang up the phone and whirl around as my mother opens the door and peeks in at me.

"Are you sick? Rowan said you were pale as a ghost."

She comes up to me and presses the back of her hand against my forehead.

I give her a weak smile. "I'm okay now. I guess I forgot to eat lunch today. And I got dizzy there for a minute. But I had some juice and a sandwich. Sorry about that." I'm saying sorry a lot lately.

"No fever. You just rest for a bit," she says. "Dad's cooking, I'm helping Rowan. Mary's here. We're covered. You need a break." She smiles at me. "Go watch some TV."

I glance at the TV, still on. "Thanks," I say.

She closes the door and disappears. I hear her stepping unevenly down the stairs, and I wonder how she takes it. The hoarding. How she doesn't crack, being married to him.

And then the phone rings right next to me and I nearly hit the ceiling. I look at the caller ID and wait for the name to come up.

It's Angotti's Trattoria.

Ten

I panic. Did he hit the call button on his caller ID by accident? If I answer, I'll look desperate. What does he want? I'm sure it's a mistake, and I imagine the awkward conversation that would follow.

Hello?

Um . . . oops. Wrong number. Hit "last call" by mistake.

Okay, bye.

Yeah. Bye.

Weird. Awful. After six rings, it stops.

I wait a minute more, and then scroll through the caller ID list. Stare at his number, then reluctantly hit delete, and it feels like the breakup we never really had. But if Dad sees that, he'll freak.

And then I go back to the TV.

I rewind the show to the commercial, and just like last time, the scene appears. I watch it over and over in slow motion. There's the snowplow, the parking lot, the building with the window just before the crash. This time I pause the scene here. There are blinds on the big window, but they are open. I see shapes—people's upper bodies. And hanging light fixtures.

The upper half of the building looks like an apartment. There are several smaller windows up there, all curtained, but I can tell lights are on. I can't make out what the words on the building say—they are mostly cut off from the frame. I go to the next frame, and the next, and the next. I can't figure out why everything has to explode—why the truck doesn't just crumple instead.

When I get to the newer part, with the fire and the wider shot, I pause again and stare at the TV. There are a few cars in the parking lot, but they are hard to make out in the dark. The only distinguishing feature I can see is the awning that's dangling there from the explosion. I can't even tell what color it is because of the smoke and shadows and the snow, but it definitely has wide stripes.

Like a restaurant awning would have.

An Italian restaurant.

I sigh deeply and squeeze my eyes shut, massaging the lids. I've been avoiding this thought, not wanting to face it. But nothing else makes sense. I don't remember ever being behind Angotti's before. We just never go there, for obvious reasons. But I think the vision is showing me the back of their restaurant. From memory, I can only picture the front of it, but even now, as many times as I've been past it, I don't remember if they have an awning out front that might be a matching counterpart of the one in the vision. I don't remember if there are apartments above the retail shops on that street or not. I can picture their sign and logo no problem—that part's etched into my brain. But the other details . . . I just don't know. I watch it to the end, and then turn off the TV and sit in the dark and think.

All I know is what I've been avoiding all along. These visions, or scenes, or whatever they are, are getting more and more frequent, and showing up in more places all the time. Obviously Sawyer isn't in a body bag. So either that means I'm insane, or it means this hasn't happened yet. I am seeing the future, and the only reason I can think of for why this is happening is that I'm supposed to do something about it. The vision is badgering me, trying to get my attention.

I guess I'm supposed to warn them, those nine people, even though I don't know who eight of them are, and get them out of there. All by myself.

Either that or I'm the biggest nutcase in the history of this family.

• • •

After a while I get my notepad and a pencil and I turn the TV back on. I don't have to go looking for the scene now—it's right there. I pause it at the wide shot where I have the best view of the whole building, searching for any street signs or other landmarks. I argue with myself. Truthfully, I don't even know if this place is in Melrose Park, or in Chicago, or even in the United States. But instinctively, I know where it has to be if there's going to be a dead Sawyer Angotti in a body bag outside.

I sketch the back of the building—what's left of it, anyway. Then I shove the sketch in my pocket, turn off the TV, grab my coat, and head downstairs. I pause before opening the door and look out the window.

The pizza delivery car is gone. I debate—if I go inside the restaurant, I'll have to wait tables. I look at the meatball truck and there's no question—I can't be seen in that tonight, lurking around. I call Trey's cell.

"What's up?" he says.

"Where are you?"

"On the way back. You feeling okay?"

"Yeah, fine—just needed some air. Can I do deliveries?"

He's quiet for a second, and I know he's trying to figure out why I'm asking. "Is this, like, your 'getting back on the horse' moment?" He's not joking. I almost got robbed—and who knows what else—last time I delivered. And even though it was a really weird situation and crime is normally not that bad here, I haven't wanted to do deliveries since then.

"Yeah, I guess it is."

"Okay," he says. I can tell he's not sure.

"I'll be fine. It was just a fluke. I need to do this to prepare for the Super Bowl tomorrow, 'cause I'm helping you. I just decided."

He hesitates. "Just make sure you do what I told you if anything happens."

"I will, I promise." I smile. He told me to kick 'em in the meatballs. "You're the best."

"I know," he says. "Now, go check the next order and make sure it's a good neighborhood—I'm pulling into the alley now."

"Got it." I hang up and go into the restaurant. I see the delivery bag on the warming shelf by the door, check the address to make sure I know where it is, and without anybody noticing me, I grab it and meet Trey at the car.

He gives me a weird look. "Is it in a good neighborhood?" he asks.

"Yeah," I say, showing him the ticket. "I'll be safe." I look him in the eye so he knows I'm not lying. "I have my phone and my keys." I show him how I stick the keys between my fingers so I can punch and gore somebody's eyes out. "And my meatball kicker," I add, wiggling my boot. I am seriously prepared.

He seems satisfied. "And Mom and Dad are good with this?"

I open my mouth to say yes, but I can't lie to him, so I just close it again.

He shakes his head at me and sighs. "Just go. Pizza's getting cold."

"Thank you." I hop in the car as he turns to go inside.

"If anything happens to you, they'll blame me," he calls out. "Do you really want that guilt hanging over you?"

I smile a little so he knows I heard him and close the door, drive down the alley. My mind is not on getting robbed. I head straight to Angotti's and pull down the side street, into the back parking lot.

When I stop the car and take a good, long look at the building in front of me, I don't need the sketch in my pocket to confirm it.

This building is going to explode.

Eleven

But when? And what am I supposed to do, wander around telling people to stay away from Angotti's because it's gonna blow?

I point my headlights at the building, and with the aid of the streetlights and building lamps, plus the light coming through the restaurant windows, I stare at it, thinking about the scene I've watched dozens of times.

There's the evergreen-and-white-striped awning, solidly attached above the back entrance. The windows above, definitely an apartment—probably where Sawyer and his parents live, just like our family. There's a glow up there, maybe from night-lights or a hallway light left on while they work the wedding reception.

I look into the wide restaurant window and see happy

people at the tables, but all I can think about is the truck crashing into them and the glass flying. I see Sawyer walk past like a blur, but I know that walk, that flip of his head, that easy, tossed-off smile that charms all the teachers. Not me—only the crooked, real smile charms me. I think about it, think about him, and my stomach quakes so hard that an aftershock runs down my thighs.

I swallow hard. "Don't die," I whisper. But I don't know how to save him.

In my head I check off everything that's supposed to be in this picture. The only things I don't see are the light fixtures hanging down over the window tables. But they probably had to hook them up to the ceiling to change the seating arrangement for the special event. And I realize that probably means it won't happen tonight, at least. A shuddering sigh escapes my throat, and I realize I've been so tensed up, I barely have a neck anymore. I drop my shoulders and take a breath, trying to shake it off.

I glance at the pizza next to me, knowing I've got to get it delivered before the customer calls to complain— that would make Trey freak out. I take one last look at the building. Even faded, the black words painted on the side are clear without the veil of snow: "Angotti's Trattoria, est. 1934." A year before ours. They've always been a step ahead of us, and we've been chasing them ever since.

I look for one last glimpse of Sawyer, but he's

nowhere to be seen, and then drive out of the parking lot to deliver this pizza. Luckily, the roads are good and I hit almost all the lights green. I call Trey and get his voice mail. "I'm on the way back. No problems."

Biggest lie of the century.

In the middle of the night the vision runs through my dreams. I startle and sit straight up in bed, wide awake, with one thought on my mind. Snow. "Oh my God," I say. "Don't be so stupid, Jules." In the scene, it's snowing.

In her bed, Rowan lifts her head off the pillow, and I can see her sleepy face scrunch up, confused. "Huh?"

I glance at her, but my mind is occupied. "Sorry. Go to sleep."

Obediently, she drops her head back on the pillow and is asleep again a moment later. I sneak out to the living room, move a pile of newspapers from the desk chair, and flip on the computer, hoping the sound is on mute like it's supposed to be. It takes forever, but finally the page loads. I dim the screen light and search for the weather forecast.

When I find it, I pull up the extended forecast and all I can do is stare. There's a chance of snow nine out of the next ten days.

"Wow. That's just great." I'm so disgusted I turn the computer off without shutting it down properly, which would really piss Rowan off. And then I just sit there in the dark, wondering how much time I have to solve this life-or-death puzzle.

And wondering how I'm going to convince people who hate us that I'm trying to save their lives . . . because I saw a vision. A vision of their restaurant, which supposedly my family has hated for generations, exploding.

Yeah, that's going to be easy.

Twelve

When I get up in the morning, I hardly have time to think about it, because today is one of the busiest Sundays on the pizza delivery calendar. Super Bowl.

Mom and Dad and Rowan go to mass. Trey and I won't go anymore out of protest—if the church won't accept my brother, they can't have me, either. Mom and Dad support our decision. I wish they'd join us. But old habits are hard to break, and their religious fear runs deep. They'll come around eventually, I think—I mean, we don't really talk about it. They're not horrible like some parents. But it still hurts Trey. Rowan wants to stay home in protest too, but they won't let her until she's sixteen, and then she can decide.

But I don't have time to think about that, either.

Trey and I get our homework done and meet Tony in the restaurant at ten to start making dough and chopping vegetables. My mind wanders as we work in silence, everybody a little sleepy this morning. I wonder if Sawyer is doing the same thing as I am today.

Sometimes I picture him and me working in a kitchen together like this, and we'd be laughing and flirting and leaving sweet little messages to each other on the cutting board in words made from green pepper slices. And I hate when I do that, because it hurts so much when reality comes crashing down on my little scene. It always does. I wish I could stop liking him. God! I just can't. I pulverize the hell out of a mushroom and have to put my knife down for a minute before I cut all my fingers off.

"Everything okay over there?" Tony asks. "I feel sorry for your cutting board. He didn't mean anything by it."

I grin. "Yeah, everything's great." I shake my hands, letting the anxiety flow out of them, and pick up the knife again.

Angotti's is bigger and has more employees than we do. I think Sawyer has two older brothers, but Sawyer is the only one left living at home, and I'm not sure if his brothers still work there. All I know is that Sawyer doesn't have to work quite as many nights as I do, because

I overhear him at school talking about places he's gone. Dances he's been to. Parties, and stuff like that. But I bet he's working today.

I shouldn't say I *have to* work as much as I do. Mom would give me a night off anytime if I asked. But I don't have a life or really many friends—no close friends, anyway, unless you count Trey. So I figure I may as well earn some tips for college, because there won't be enough money to go around for all three of us.

Today I'm actually kind of excited to work. It's my first Super Bowl doing delivery. I remember last year Trey was insane. Our cousin Nick—Mary's son—helped out as a backup driver like he does sometimes. This year, the backup driver is me. Last night, after my successful delivery, I told my mom I was ready. She was a little skeptical, but I think I convinced her I'm fine, so she called Nick and told him he had the night off, which he seemed really happy about.

So they need me. By the time Mom, Dad, and Rowan get down to the restaurant after mass, the phone is ringing off the hook with big preorders for later.

It's funny—sometimes I see how it is at fast-food restaurants and on those reality cooking shows when the aspiring chefs are slammed and yelled at constantly. Everybody's running around, not communicating, and it's supertense. Usually somebody's barking out orders—and everybody hates that guy. Here at Demarco's we sort of go into superhero mode when we're slammed, and it's really pretty fun. Today, Trey and I play a game to try to get Rowan to laugh when she's on the phone, because if we can really get her going, she'll snort. "Hey, Trey, do you wanna see—" I say.

"Harry Potter?"

"No—"

"Boobies?"

I crack up, and Tony shakes his head and gives a reluctant laugh, but Rowan stays concentrated on her phone order. She's always been wound up pretty tight, and it takes a while to get her loose enough. Apparently today is not that day. By the time the lunch crowd dwindles and we're all in the kitchen stocking up supplies and making boxes and chopping more veggies, Rowan is answering call after call, ignoring us while we're making dumb "dot-com" and "that's what she said" jokes after every twelve-inch meatball sub order she reads back.

Yet, in the back of my mind, I'm agonizing. Wondering if tonight is the night.

When it's time to start, we get serious. "I'll take the east-side deliveries," I say to Trey. "I know the streets better." I lean against the door with my first loaded-up pizza sweater—that's what Tony calls the insulating bag.

Trey shrugs, distracted by the crap ton of orders that

are piling up. "That's fine. We need to move it. Don't speed, but don't linger."

"I know," I say. "I'm heading out." With a wave, I push out the back door into the cold, snowy afternoon. I try to drive by Angotti's every chance I get.

Thirteen

The afternoon flies by. Mom keeps up with the few tables in the dining room, and Rowan stays in the back pulling pizzas out of the oven, cutting them and boxing them up, keeping watch out the back door so she can see us coming and run them out to us so we don't have to park and come in for our next load.

The slick roads are slowing us down. I'm not afraid to drive in snow, but it's frustrating when customers don't understand that weather is a factor in how fast we get the food out. But the upside is that the later into the evening we get, the drunker the customers get, and for most of them that means they tip more.

I manage to drive by Angotti's twice even though I really don't have time, and everything looks okay inside. If the crash is going to happen tonight, there's nothing I can do about it. And somehow, in the midst of all this driving and thinking today, I realize that I absolutely *do* have to do something about this. I have to tell Sawyer. Because what if this vision thing is not just a big weird nothing? What if something really happens to him? To all nine of them? How's that going to make me feel for the rest of my life? It would be worse to do nothing and feel horrible forever than to say something and make a temporary fool out of myself. And, hell, maybe I am nuts. Maybe I just need to do that one over-the-edge cry-for-help thing that'll get my illness noticed and give me the treatment I apparently need. That's what all the experts say on TV, you know. Here's my big blaring chance to be heard.

I head toward Traverse Apartments, which is across the street from where "the incident" happened on Christmas Eve. My thoughts turn to that night, that walk through the shadows of the apartment complex trying to find 93B, that prickly feeling at the back of my neck and the sweat that came out of nowhere when I heard pounding feet and felt the guy grab my coat.

It all went really fast. The guy shoved my pizza bag up at my face and slung his arm around my neck, staying behind me so I couldn't see him. He ripped my little money belt off me and shoved me into a snowy bush, face-first. And then I heard a click of a knife by my ear.

I couldn't even scream—my throat was paralyzed. My whole body was paralyzed. I was so scared I couldn't even react to wipe the burning snow from my face. I was like some stupid bunny in the street when he sees the lights of an oncoming car and waits for a tire tread to hit him in the face.

I heard a door slam and a rush of footsteps as apparently some stranger came flying out of one of the buildings and tackled the guy. They rolled around while I scrambled to wipe the snow off my face, and the mugger managed to get up and get away. The stranger chased after him, and I never saw either one of them again.

I wasn't hurt, and I wasn't much help to the police. It had been really dark, and I didn't get a look at the mugger's face, didn't really have a concept of how big a dude he was. The police guessed it was probably a random incident— some meth addict who needed money for supplies and was waiting for anybody to come along.

I shake away the memory and squint at the signs in this complex until I find the right building and a parking spot nearby. I don't give myself time to get nervous, I just grab the warmer bag, zip out of the car. I jog up the three steps to the building and nearly wipe out on a slick spot right by the door, where a bunch of icicles must drip during the day and make a big ice patch on the step at night.

When I grab the door handle to steady myself, it swings open hard, right at me, knocking into the corner of my pizza bag and sending it sliding off my gloved fingers just as somebody plows out of the building into me, more startling than scary.

Out of instinct I reach out as I fall back, my focus on catching the pizza bag rather than on how I'll land, and it's one of those slow-motion moments where everything is blurry, my hands won't move where I want them to, and my body is going in the opposite direction from the way I want it to go. Meanwhile, whoever plowed into me is now tripping over my leg and falling too . . . and his shoulder or arm or something takes my precious red bag with it.

My elbow takes the worst hit when I land, then my back, and my head smacks on the cement, but I'm wearing a hat so it's cushioned, thank the dogs. The wind rushes out of me and I lie there for a moment trying to get it back, stunned. Immediately I think it's another attack, but there's no menacing feeling here. A second later I'm sure it's just an unfortunate collision.

"Shit," I hear. "I'm sorry."

I try to sit up, and flames shoot through my arm, tears of pain and frustration over the lost merchandise and lost time starting to sting. My pizza bag rests upside down in the snow about five feet away. I close my eyes. "Shit," I echo. My brain rushes to calculate the time wasted. At least forty minutes before I can get back here again with a fresh pizza. Maybe thirty-five . . .

"Are you okay?"

I freeze as it registers: I know that voice. And now I can't speak at all, because Sawyer Angotti is tossing his empty pizza bag aside and kneeling on the icy step next to me. And I'm furious.

Five reasons why I, Jules Demarco, am furious:
1. The pizza I was ten feet away from delivering
   properly is now something only Trey
   would eat
2. My stupid wenus* is broken and hurts like hell
3. It's a snowy Super Bowl Sunday and I'm
   already running forty-five minutes behind
4. Some loser (even though I'm in love with him)
   wasn't watching where he was going, and I'm
   the one who has to suffer for it
5. That loser just delivered *his* pizza without
   consequence, and also? Does not have a
   broken wenus

"I'm fine," I manage to say. Embarrassed, I ignore the pain, roll away from his outstretched hand, and get

---

*look it up

to my feet, holding my sore elbow close to my side. I reach out and gingerly pick up my pizza bag. I close my eyes once again and swallow hard. The inside of that box will be pretty gross right now. I don't want to think about it.

"I'm really sorry—I was in a hurry . . ."

It's true that he's being ridiculously nice about this. I almost wish he weren't. If he were a jerk about it, I could stay furious a lot longer.

"Me too," I confess with a sigh. "I was already off balance from the ice when you barreled through the door." *Shut up, shut up,* I tell myself. Now I'm mad at myself for taking part of the blame. *What the hell, Jules?*

It's love! I cry back to myself. *How can I help it?*

I hate you, I say to inner Jules. *Hate. You.*

Sawyer cringes when he sees how not-floppy my bag is. "Oooh. Been there. Sorry. I really am," he says. He dips his head and looks into my eyes.

"Yeah. Thanks." I've dropped a few pizzas in my day. "Not the best day for it, but there it is." All of a sudden I sound like my dad talking about the weather. I drop my eyes because I can't stand to look at him being nice, knowing what I know.

"Want me to pay for it?" Sawyer comes to life and whips out a wad of tips from his pocket, and all I can do is stare at him.

"Who *are* you?" I say, almost under my breath, but he hears me, and I see his lips twitch.

"I'm just a clumsy guy," he mutters. "I hope your parents don't freak out."

I narrow my eyes, not sure if he's just concerned about me dropping a pizza and getting yelled at, or if there's another layer there. "They won't," I say slowly. "Why would they? And put your money away. It's fine. It happens. Trey will eat it."

He laughs then. "So would I. You sure?" He looks at me, eye to eye again, and I remember his lashes from a long time ago when we were forced to share a library table doing research. His lashes are superthick, superlong, deep brown, complemented by the green of his irises. Every blink is a sweeping drama, a sexy ornament, a mating ritual. Dear dog, I'm so hopelessly pathetic, I'm grossing myself out.

I nod stupidly.

He shoves the money back in his pocket, and we just stand there, silent and awkward. Finally he says, "Need me to call in the reorder for you?"

That wakes me up. "Shit," I say again, and dig wildly for my phone. "No. But that would definitely make my parents freak out, if that's what you're going for."

He grins. I dial and turn away so his ropy eyelashes don't distract me. "We have a situation," I say when Rowan answers. "There's a pie down at Traverse

Apartments. Repeat: A pie. Is down. Reorder stat."

"Jules!" she says. "We don't have time for that."

"Calm it down, yo," I say, gingerly stretching out my sore arm to see if it still works. "I'll be back in fifteen so you can load me up. . . . I don't know what else to say. It happened. There was ice. Sorry."

She sighs. "Fine. Just get here."

"Roger that." I hang up and turn back to Sawyer, who is still smiling.

"Is something funny?" Now I'm back to almost furious again. I start walking to my car.

He shrugs. "It must be fun to work with you."

"Oh yeah, I'm a real hoot," I say, opening my car door and knocking my boot on the runner.

"I think you guys . . . you and Trey, and your little sister—"

"Rowan," I say automatically.

"Rowan," he says with a nod. "It's cool you all get to work together. I'm stuck with the proprietors." He says the last word with sarcasm.

And that's the moment when I picture him at the hostess stand at his parents' restaurant, by the jar of suckers, and that's when I remember the phone call, and that's when I see the body bag in my mind's eye. My mouth opens slowly, as if it's deciding whether to say the words my brain is telling it to say.

"You know . . . ," I start to say.

At the same time, Sawyer says, "About last night . . ."

And we both stop and start again.

"I shouldn't have called you," I say.

"I called you back. After."

I blink and look away. "I know."

He lifts an eyebrow. "You didn't answer."

"I thought . . ." But I can't remember anymore.

"It was nice of you," he says. "Kind of weird, but nice. I'm sorry I accused you of spying. Knee-jerk reaction. Or maybe just a jerk reaction. It was stupid."

I swallow hard, and now I picture those gorgeous lashes on his dead eyes. "Sawyer," I say, and his name sounds so weird when I say it out loud.

"I don't like this *thing*, you know," he says. "I miss . . . I mean, I wish . . ."

"I know." I look at the ground, my courage gone. He misses . . . what? He misses me? He misses the way things used to be? Did he really almost say that?

Now I can't tell him what I desperately need to say, what I told myself I'd say. Because if I do, he'll walk away from all of this thinking I'm a total mental case. And that would end everything. Every last pillow dream, every hope for that first kiss.

But he could die before any of that could ever happen. I'm so confused I don't know what's the right thing to do.

My phone buzzes in my pocket. "I have to go," I choke out.

He looks at the ground. "It's cool. I'll . . . see you?"

Dear dog, I hope so.

Fourteen

The rest of the night is a mess. Immediately every poster in every store window, every stop sign, every TV in every house I deliver to is showing me a truck crashing into Angotti's. It's like each object that is created to communicate any sort of visual message is coming alive, screaming at me to do something, to warn the victims, and they won't let up.

I can't concentrate on my orders. The Traverse Apartments fiasco put me way behind, and customers start calling to complain. Dad is overanxious and fidgety every time I drive up. Trey's trying to calm me down on the phone but I can't talk to him and drive on snow at the same time, so I just give up. I can't tell him what's wrong when he asks, even though I really wish I could. I'm getting a massive headache.

When the marquee at the Park Theatre blinks a fluorescent picture of the crash for the entire thirty seconds I'm stuck at the stoplight nearby, I think I'm going to lose it. This weird fear churns in my chest, and I can feel a flutter there, like my heart is racing, trying to urge me to go, go, go. "Stop it!" I scream from the driver's seat. I pound the steering wheel with my gloved hands. "Just stop."

But it doesn't stop. It gets worse. Every window in every house I pass has the scene plastered over it. Every poster on every telephone pole has changed its picture from whatever lost pet it was in search of to the explosion. I have to stop several times just to get a grip and figure out where the hell I'm going. I start lagging even farther behind, until it's all just so hopeless.

With one pizza to go, I can't take it anymore, because maybe all of this bombardment means the crash is happening right now, tonight. And somehow it'll be my fault.

Instead of delivering it, I turn down the street and head to Angotti's.

The building is still standing and there's plenty of parking out front. It's late, almost eleven. I call Trey and tell his voice mail that I'm fine, tell him that I have to make an extra stop and not to worry, all the while watching shadows of the Angotti's staff move from room to room through the front window. It's funny in a not-at-all-funny sort of way—this is the one window that doesn't have the explosion plastered all over it.

For a moment, watching the peaceful movement inside and for once not being bombarded with hyperexplosions at every turn, I talk myself back out of it. I think maybe I need more sleep. Maybe I just need to . . . I don't know. Talk to somebody about this vision. A professional.

The thought of telling someone what's been happening scares me to death. I imagine how they'd look at me. I imagine them pushing a panic button under their desk to summon security, or telling me they're taking me to get a Coke but really they're delivering me to doctors with white coats who will grab me and bring me to some asylum where they'll stick electrodes or whatever on my temples and armpits and do weird testing and shave my head and shit like that. And I'll have a toothless roommate who is seriously insane and who wants to kill me.

I feel my throat tighten and burn as tears run down the back of it instead of down my cheeks. I sit outside Angotti's and try to give myself a pep talk. What's the worst thing that could happen if I go inside and talk to Sawyer? In my mind, I list them.

Five bad things that could happen:
    1. I go in and tell Sawyer and he thinks I'm
       insane and tells everybody, and my life is over

2. Sawyer's parents shoot me dead on sight (not a bad option at this point, actually, now that I think about it)
3. The whole fucking crash happens and the place explodes *while I'm inside*
4. That's really all I can think of at this point because of all the panic and such
5. As if three bad things weren't enough

My phone rings while I'm sitting there, and it's Trey. I squeeze my eyes shut and take a breath, then turn off the phone and shove it into my pocket. I look over at the last delivery, growing cold on the seat next to me. "Sorry, Mrs. Rodriguez," I say. "I hope you don't stay up too late waiting for it." I wonder idly what my father will do when I get back home after not delivering it. It's weird how little I care about that now.

Finally I grab the handle and shove the car door open. I step out into the slush and close the door softly behind me, and then walk stoically toward Angotti's front door.

Fifteen

A little bell jingles when I open the door, and a beautiful, plump middle-aged woman looks up from behind the cash wrap.

"We're just closing down the kitchen," she says apologetically. And then she narrows her eyes and stares at the Demarco's Pizzeria logo on my hat. Her voice turns cold. "Can I help you?"

"Is Sawyer here?"

She doesn't answer at first. Maybe she's trying to think of an excuse. "I'll check," she says finally. She goes to the nearby swinging door and opens it a crack, never taking her eyes off me. "Sawyer," she calls out.

"Yeah, Ma?" I hear, and I look down at the carpet. *What the hell am I doing?*

"There's a young lady out here to see you."

He doesn't say anything. I imagine him pausing, wondering what amazing babe it could possibly be coming by to see him. Picturing how disappointed he'll be to see me.

He comes out and slides past his mother. His eyes open in alarm when he sees me, and he comes over. "What are you doing here?" he whispers. He looks over his shoulder at Mrs. Angotti, who is watching us very closely.

"I have to tell you something. It's really important," I say.

"It couldn't wait until school?" he asks, incredulous. "You had to come *here*?"

And now I start doubting myself again. But then I glance outside and see snow falling. Across the street, the Walk sign blinks an exploding truck. It's now or possibly never.

"It can't wait," I say simply, and look up at him.

The alarm in his eyes turns to concern. He keeps his voice low. "Let's step outside." He looks over his shoulder again at his mother and says gruffly, "I'll be right back."

I don't look at her. I don't want to see what she's thinking. I don't want to know the degrading thoughts she's had about me since before I was born. I reach for the handle and go outside. Sawyer follows me.

When the door closes, he keeps his back to the restaurant. "What the hell, Jules?" There's anger in his voice. "You can't just show up here. Not wearing that. Not at all."

I can understand why he's upset. I don't know exactly what sort of mess I've just put him in, but I can imagine the scenario in reverse, and it makes me cringe. I didn't even think about the hat. Maybe I should have called. But he was on deliveries tonight, so that wouldn't have helped. I don't have his cell number. It'd be the same mess. I take a deep breath. "Look, Sawyer. I'm sorry to do this to you. I know I'm probably causing a problem, but here's the thing." I pull off my cap and comb my fingers through my hair, trying to think.

When I don't continue, he folds his arms against the cold and shifts his weight. "Well?" he says after a moment. "Kinda cold out here."

I look at the Walk sign once more to gather strength, and then sigh and close my eyes, remembering the scene in my mind, frame by frame, landing on Sawyer's dead face. And I look back up at him, into his eyes. "You see," I say, and it sounds very grown-up in my ears. "I . . ."

"What?" he says, but the edge in his voice is fading.

"I'm just . . ." *Oh, shit. What was I thinking? What am I supposed to say here?* "I'm worried about your restaurant. I think . . . I mean, I have a weird . . . feeling . . . like something bad is going to happen. To it." *To you.*

In my best-case scenario, this is where he thanks me

and gathers me into his strong arms, and his face hovers near mine, and we kiss for the first time.

In my probable-case scenario, this is where he calls me a nutjob and tells me to go away.

In my worst-case scenario, this is where the restaurant explodes and I'm in one of the body bags.

None of those three things happens.

Sawyer just stares at me for a minute. And then his voice comes out cold. "Is your father going to sabotage us?"

"What?" I exclaim. "No! No, Sawyer."

He pulls out his phone. "Son of a bitch," he mutters.

"What are you doing?" I ask, grabbing his arm. "No. Listen to me."

He pauses. "Then, what? Are you delivering a warning from him, or a threat?"

"Oh my God," I say. "This is not happening. It's neither one, Sawyer. I'm saying everything all wrong."

"What is this, then? What's going on? Is he suing us? He doesn't stand a chance, you know."

"Sawyer," I say, and nothing is making sense. "Stop. Just hold on a second. This has nothing to do with my family! I—I have this vision . . . thing . . ." I trail off. It sounds absolutely ridiculous saying it out loud.

"What?" He looks at me like I've lost my marbles.

But now I'm committed. "I keep seeing a vision," I say,

trying to sound authoritative and not insane. "Over and over. You have to believe me, Sawyer, just listen. Please."

He stops fingering his phone, gently pulls his arm away from my grasp, and takes a step away from me. "A vision," he says sarcastically.

My heart sinks. I look away. In the window of the apartment across the street, I watch the scene and explain it as it happens. "Yes," I say in a quiet voice. "It's snowing pretty hard. A snowplow comes careening over the curb into your back parking lot. It hits the restaurant. There's a huge explosion." I turn back to him. "People die." I close my lips. *You, you, you, Sawyer. You die.*

He doesn't react, waiting for more.

"Obviously I'm aware that I sound crazy," I say evenly, realizing my life is now over. "I can't explain why it's happening. I don't ever have visions otherwise, and I don't think I'm insane. I just keep seeing this—on billboards and TVs and stop signs and . . ." I trail off and face him once more, trying to keep my stupid quivering lip from betraying me. "I just felt like I had to tell you, because if I didn't, and something happened to you . . . your restaurant, I mean, I wouldn't be able to forgive myself." *And by the way, I love you.*

He stands there a long moment, his eyes narrowed, snow falling and sticking to his hair and lashes. He blinks the flakes away.

"Look," I say, and I make my voice sound clinical now to keep myself from losing it. "I never expected you to believe me. I just had to say something. For me." And suddenly I know it's over, and I've done my job, and that's all I have. I nod once very quickly and add, "That's it," as if to signal an end to the insanity, and then turn away and walk to my car.

He doesn't stop me.

I get in and start it up, letting the windshield wipers take care of the snow and the defroster clear up the steamy glass caused by cooling pizza. All the while I pray for my door to magically open, for him to come after me. But I'm so afraid to look. Finally, when I start to appear either desperate or suspicious from sitting there so long, I pull out of the parking spot and dare to look back. He's still standing outside, watching me go. Gathered at the storefront window now, and peering out at me, are Sawyer's mother and two men. Next to her is a man I recognize as Sawyer's father, and next to him is an elderly mustachioed man. And as all the thoughts of what I've just done numb my brain, I realize that the old gentleman standing there must be the infamous Mr. Fortuno Angotti—the man whose caricatured face adorns the Angotti's sauce label. The man who stole our family's recipe and drove my grandfather to his grave.

Sixteen

Rowan meets me at the door. "Dad's freaking out," she says.

"Tough."

"What's that?" Rowan points at my bag.

"I messed up."

"Is that your last order?"

"Yep, sure is."

Rowan grabs it and pulls the box out. "It's . . . moist."

"Yup." I shrug. I feel like crying. I've totally messed up two orders in one night. Not cool. Not to mention that other thing.

"The kitchen is already shut down, Jules. What do you plan to do? Where have you been all this time?"

"Lost in the blizzard. Couldn't find it." I can't look at

her. I move past her and go to the sink to wash my hands and splash some water on my face.

"Dad's gonna shit a brick."

I push my fingers into my eyes, trying to stop the guilty tears from coming. But everything is so stupid. Why did I say anything? By tomorrow, everybody at school will know I'm a mental case. Sawyer must think I'm a freak.

"Are you okay?" Rowan asks, looking at me hard. Her voice softens. "Oh my gosh, are you crying? Seriously, you don't have to cry about it."

I grab blindly for a paper towel, determined not to make a single cry noise. I blow the sob out through my lips, nice and slow, and breathe in.

"Although," Rowan says, musing to herself, "I would probably cry if it were me. I hate not finishing the job, you know? Makes me feel like a total failure."

I take another deep breath and pull the towel away from my face. "You're not helping."

Trey bursts in the door with his empty bag, whistling. "Major tips, girlie," he says to Rowan, flapping his wad of money in her face.

"You have to share, you know."

"Not on Super Bowl Sunday," he says, teasing her. He notices the pizza box sitting there and looks at me. "What happened?"

"She got lost," Rowan says. "Jules, did you call the people? You had their number."

I don't want to lie anymore. "No. I just messed up, okay? Can you call them?"

Trey gives me a weird look but says nothing.

Rowan sighs deeply and grabs the phone, then looks at the ticket on the box and starts punching buttons. "Fine," she mutters. "It's, like, eleven p.m., my gosh, and—Oh, hi! This is Rowan from Demarco's Pizzeria. We are sooo sorry—"

I flee through the kitchen to the dining room. May as well face the wrath and get it over with.

Mom is rolling napkins.

"Where's Dad?" I ask.

"Upstairs. Very upset." She looks at me like she's waiting for something.

"Sorry about dropping that pizza earlier and messing everything up. I, ah . . ."

"You're fine," she says, waving it off. "But why don't you tell me what else you did?"

I stare at her. "What do you mean?"

"You know."

I hate when she does this. It's like she's trying to trick me into confessing things, which really pisses me off because I'm a good kid. I sigh. She couldn't possibly know about this most recent pizza fiasco yet, could she?

She's freaking jiggy with her ESP. "Mother, please. I'm tired."

She presses her lips together, and then says, "Your father got a call about ten minutes ago from Mario Angotti."

The implications are so heavy, so unexpected, I can't even speak. I sit down hard in a chair and put my face in my hands. "Who?"

She glares. "Mario Angotti. Son of Fortuno Angotti. Father of Sawyer Angotti, whose acquaintance I believe you've made."

"Oh, no," I whisper. "Oh, mother-fuh-lovin' crap." I can't believe they called. I didn't do anything. "No-o," I moan as it all sinks in. I can't look at my mother. "What did he say?"

"He said, 'Anthony, keep your riffraff out of my restaurant or I'll slap a restraining order on your whole family.' Or something like that."

"Wait. He said 'riffraff'?"

"It might have been another word."

"Oh." I rub my sore elbow and shake my head, staring at the ancient carpet. "How's Dad handling it?"

Mom gives me a rueful smile and reaches for another stack of napkins. "I think you can probably guess."

I stand up and start pacing around the tables. "Crap," I mutter. "What now?"

"Why on earth did you go there, Julia?"

I stop pacing and look at her. "I had to tell Sawyer something. He's the one who knocked my pizza over earlier . . ." I don't know what I'm saying anymore. All I know is that I should probably stop talking.

"He knocked your pizza over? On purpose?"

"No! Nothing like that. It was an accident."

"What kind of hooligan would do that? We should be the ones slapping a restraining order on *him*," she says.

Oh, hey, there's a way to ruin my life even more. "Please, please don't do that."

"We just might."

"Well, that's great." I get up and grab my gloves. "I'm going to bed."

I stomp into the kitchen just as Trey pulls a pizza out of the oven. "Is that the one I messed up on? They still want it, this late?"

"Yep," he says. He cuts it, grabs a box and slides it in, then maneuvers it into the bag.

I'm so frustrated I want to punch the wall. "Okay, awesome," I say. "I'll be back in twenty minutes." I reach for the bag.

"I got it," he says. "Go upstairs."

I bite my lip. He makes me want to cry. I know I should object, but I don't. "You won't believe what I did," I say.

"Probably not." He smiles and grabs his coat and keys,

then the pizza, and he's out the door. "Wait up, we'll talk. It'll be fine," he calls as it closes.

"Thanks, Trey. I will," I say, but he's gone. All I can hear now is Dad slinging crap around upstairs. I head out of the restaurant as Trey's taillights disappear, and start making my way upstairs to deal with Dad.

Seventeen

When I enter the apartment, Dad is fuming. At
first, he just looks at me and shakes his head—it's the
Demarco way of exuding disappointment without a word,
and it works. The irony here is that he's standing in the
middle of the dining room, next to where I think there
might be a table and some chairs somewhere, but they've
been loaded with piles and piles of his junk for the past
nine years. Yet nobody ever calls him on that.

His silence is thick. Finally I speak up. "I'm sorry I
went to Angotti's. I just had to tell—"

"No!" His voice thunders, and he starts in. "You do
not 'just have to' anything with the Angottis. Ever. Do
you hear me? Do you want to ruin our business? You want
the newspaper to find out that the Angottis have put a

restraining order on the Demarcos? What does that say to the community?"

"They haven't done that—"

He starts pointing at me. "Not yet. Not yet. Better be never. You stay away from that boy. Do I need to find a new school for you? Is that it?"

My jaw drops. As much as I dislike my school, at least I have Trey and Rowan there. At least I can look at Sawyer once a day. "Dad, seriously! Are you really trying to ruin my life?"

He gives me a suspicious look. "What are you doing with him?"

"Nothing! I swear."

"Then why do you have to tell him something?"

I take a breath and go with the first thing I can come up with. "School project. We're on a team. The teacher assigned us."

He narrows his eyes, but I can tell he wants to believe me. "What class?"

"Psych," I say. It's almost not a lie.

"You stay away from that place," he says once more.

"I will, Dad. I'm sorry."

When I wake up Monday morning after a terrible night's sleep, I fight off all the thoughts about what could still happen to Sawyer. I can't deal with that right now.

All I can think about is that I did what I had to do. I warned him. And just because everything's all turmoily, and my dad's a messed-up freak, and the boy I L.O.V.E. probably thinks I belong in an asylum, doesn't change the fact that I have now satisfied whatever weird business has been going on in my head, and I am now free. I yank open the curtains and look out at the windows across the street. None of them show me an explosion. I cross my fingers and hope it's over.

I also hope Sawyer won't tell the whole world what I said to him. But the chances of this? Zero.

And Dad's just going to have to get over it.

Five insanely overdramatic things I heard Dad muttering to himself last night as he paced the hallway outside my room:
1. "You have betrayed the name of Demarco!"
   (Yo, Shakespeare, live in the now)
2. "Why couldn't you just deliver the pizza to my dear friends?" (So you and Mrs. Rodriguez are hanging out now?)
3. "Now look what you've done. You've fired the first shot!" (WTF?)
4. "No more deliveries for you. We'll hire a boy." (Oh, *o*-kay)
5. "Why do you want to break my heart?" (big sigh)

And now I'm grounded for two weeks, which is no big deal because I don't go anywhere anyway. The worse punishment is that I've got to go to school and face the impending ridicule.

I brush my teeth and touch some pink gloss to my lips as Trey hangs on the other side of the bathroom door, waiting to get in, and I realize I'm the one who should be furious. After all, I bet Sawyer could have stopped his dad from calling my dad.

"He must think I'm a total nutball," I murmur as I swipe a little raisin-colored eyeliner under my lower lashes.

"I totally do," Trey says through the crack in the door. "Can you move it along? My hair needs clay before it dries like this. I practically have a 'fro."

I open the door and he stumbles in over a new pile of magazines that surfaced since last night.

"You okay?" he asks. He got home during the muttering portion of my fight with Dad, and I'd filled him in on the rest, except of course for the real reason why I had to go see Sawyer. And I get the feeling Trey thinks there's something relational going on between Sawyer and me . . . which I'm happy to go along with.

"Yeah, I'm okay," I say in a low voice. "It's just so stupid." And the bigger part of me that can't deal with the truth is crying out the thing I'm not quite ready to acknowledge. That even though I warned Sawyer, he could still die if he doesn't do anything about what I told him.

Trey sculpts his hair expertly and whispers, "What's a girl in love supposed to do? In the movies, she has to defy Daddy someday. Yesterday was your day. The first of many, I suppose." He sighs. "And we're all in for more yelling. Great."

"No, I'm done with it. No more yelling."

He washes his hands and looks at me in the mirror. "Yeah, right."

"Really," I say, putting my things in the drawer as Rowan bursts in and squeezes between us. "It's not worth this. I'll . . . just forget about him."

"Forget about who?" she asks. She slept through the fight last night.

"Nobody," Trey and I say together.

Rowan shoves my shoulder. "You guys are so mean. Move it. It's my turn in here."

Trey and I escape. He takes off to meet Carter for his ride to school, and I cautiously flip on the TV while I wait for Rowan to finish getting ready. I watch a full five-minute weather segment plus commercials, with no sign of any explosions anywhere. And a bonus—the forecast changed, like it tends to do around here. Now the weatherwoman is predicting clear skies for two days.

"Big sigh," I whisper, and I'm flooded with relief. I really think it's over. Even if I'm about to be known at my high school as the weirdest freak on the planet, at least I'm not truly insane. And at the very least, if Sawyer dies, it won't be my fault.

Jeez. What kind of sick person thinks like that?

Eighteen

On the billboard, I see Jose Cuervo for the first time in weeks. It's the most hopeful-looking thing I've ever seen in my life. "I love you, Jose," I say as we pass it. Rowan doesn't hear me. She's got her earbuds in, listening to something while she layers on more makeup in the sun visor mirror.

"Hey," I say, poking her in the shoulder when we're stopped at a light.

She pulls an earbud out. "What? Don't freaking bump me." She wipes lip gloss off her chin and starts over.

"Sorry. I just wondered how you're doing."

Rowan turns her head and frowns. "What?"

I laugh and shake my head. "Why are you suddenly so into makeup? Do you have a boyfriend?"

Her mouth opens like she's going to say something, then she closes it and says, "No," in a voice that doesn't want to be questioned further. She puts her earbud back in.

"Okay." I feel a little twinge in my heart for her. And then I picture us as spinsters living together forever, her being all sweet one minute and grouchy the next, her face perfectly made up just in case, and me leaving myself notes with sliced-vegetable lettering on the cutting board.

As usual, I ditch Rowan once we get to school—not that she minds—and keep my head down, avoiding eyes. Avoiding anyone talking with anyone else, because I'm pretty sure they're talking about me. I don't even dare take my usual glance to where Sawyer should be standing. Instead, I just stare into my locker and wait for the first whispers to reach my ears.

I grab the books I need and give myself a little pep talk, then slam the locker door and head to first hour. I keep my eyes on the floor, shoulders curved inward, and travel through the crowded hallway like a lithe bumble-bee, zigging and zagging and curving around people, one purpose in mind—getting through the morning, one period at a time. Then the dreaded lunch hour, and finally the afternoon.

And I make it through okay, only once narrowly avoiding Sawyer when I see him coming toward me after school. I duck into Mr. Polselli's psych classroom until he passes.

"Hi," Mr. Polselli says. He's grading papers at his desk.

"Oh, hi," I say.

"How's your paper coming along?"

I totally haven't started it. "Fine."

"What's your topic?"

"Um, I think, maybe, I'm not quite ready to tell you yet," I say with a guilty grin.

He laughs. "I see."

"But I do have a question. About a . . . possible topic. If a person, like, sees visions or whatever, does that mean they're, you know, insane, or crazy or anything?"

"Depends."

"Oh."

"It could mean that. But it might not."

"Oh. Well, do you know if . . . if people who see visions, do those visions ever, like, happen?"

"What do you mean?"

"Like can people see something in the future and know something's going to happen, and then it actually happens?"

He tilts his head and looks at me over his reading glasses. "Where are you headed with this? You mean like fortune-tellers? Psychics?"

I look at the floor, which has black scuff marks all over it. "I guess."

"There's a lot of debate about that. You could *probably* do some research on it and find out, you know."

I nod. "Okay. Yeah, I know. I will. Thanks."

"Anytime."

"See you tomorrow."

Mr. Polselli smiles and pushes his glasses up, resuming his grading. I check the hallway to be sure Sawyer is gone and make my way to the parking lot.

When I round the corner of the building, I run into him. Not literally, thank dog. But now that I think of it, I owe him a crash.

He's standing next to his car, his door open and his arm draped over it, talking to two of the girls—Roxie and Sarah—who were in my family's restaurant the night Angotti's was closed for the wedding reception. He's giving them that charming smile.

I stop short, then divert my path to get to my giant meatball truck, which is so inconspicuous I'm sure no one will notice me driving it out of here. I glance at him and he's looking at me, frowning, talking to the girls. They turn my way, and I barrel down a row of cars to the back of the parking lot, my face burning.

Rowan is standing—no, hopping—outside the truck, waiting for me. "Finally!" she says. Then she narrows her eyes and looks past me. "What does he want?"

I turn around, and Sawyer's jogging toward me. Alone.

My eyes pop open and I get this twisty thing in my gut. I look at Rowan. "Get in the truck," I say, unlocking her door. "Now."

"Sheesh," she says, but she gets in and closes the door, then stares at us. I turn my back to her as Sawyer slows to a walk a few feet away.

I shift my weight to one hip and lean against the door. "What."

He stops and flips his car keys around his finger a few times. His breath comes out in a cloud. "Yeah, um, sorry my dad freaked out and called your dad. I couldn't stop him."

I just look at him and hug my books to my chest. "My dad flipped out."

"I figured."

"I shouldn't have gone to your place."

He shrugs. "You're pro'ly right."

"I told my dad it was for an assignment for psych class."

He drops his gaze and gets that half grin on his face. "I'm not actually taking psych."

"Great." I'm such an idiot. I squint at the snow-covered pavement, which is brighter than white today because the sun's actually out. It's cold enough that it hasn't melted. But heat climbs up my neck to my cheeks when I think about how mad my father was.

Sawyer kicks a hunk of dirty snow from under my truck and says nothing.

"So, okay, then," I say. Every second that passes, I feel more and more stupid, and I don't like the lump that's forming in my throat. I try to clear it, but I can't control it. It's getting bigger. "I guess I don't really need the drama," I say, "of a . . . a re*strain*ing order, y'know, against my whole *fam*ily." The words are getting louder as an anger I didn't know I had builds up inside me.

He looks at me with alarm, neither one of us expecting this, but I can't stop. "So I guess after all those years of secret friendship, which you totally threw in the trash after I, like, was so scary that I *smiled* at you in public, in front of your dad, and then had the *audacity* to enter your restaurant almost four years later and throw everybody into a wild fit . . . well, I guess I'll just see you, you know, *never*. Oh, and thanks for telling everybody I'm insane." I reach blindly for the truck door and open it.

"Jesus, Jules." His arm shoots out and he pushes the door shut. "I said I'm sorry. And . . . holy shit, I don't really know what to say about all of that in the middle there . . . I—I didn't know you ever thought about that anymore." He blinks his long stupid lashes at me. "But I promise I didn't tell anybody you're insane." He steps back and straightens his jacket collar. "I figured it was, I don't know. Just weird."

Angry tears burn at the corners of my eyes, and I will them with all my might not to fall. I glance through the window at Rowan, who's sitting up, looking like she's ready to jump out of the vehicle and attack. I shake my head at her, trying to reassure her with a shaky smile. "Okay, fine," is all I can think of to say. He thinks I'm weird. "I need to go."

"And I—don't know what to say about the rest."

"Yeah. You said that." I reach for the door handle again.

"So, you know, *are* you?" He shoves his dangly keys into his coat pocket suddenly and coughs.

I look at him. "Am I . . . what?"

His face is red and he can't look at me. "Never mind. I'm an idiot. See you." He turns to go.

And then I get it. "Am I insane? Is that what you mean?"

"Forget it, Jules. It was a stupid thing to say," he says over his shoulder as he starts walking.

"Oh my God!"

He walks faster to his car. And I stand here like a total loser, watching him go.

I don't blame him. He doesn't believe me. I never expected him to believe me.

And he's obviously right in thinking that.

• • •

From that moment, I'm bombarded with the vision once again—my peace didn't even last twenty-four hours. I drive home and every stop sign, every store window, and the billboard are covered in the scene of the crash. Rowan tries to find out what's going on, but I drive in stony silence. Eventually she's smart enough to shut up.

When we pull in the alley where we park the beast, Trey is standing there waiting where he always is so we can keep up our "all going to school in the giant truck of balls" ruse. I turn off the engine and look hard at Rowan. "Don't you ever tell Mom and Dad that I was anywhere near Sawyer Angotti, you hear me?"

Her eyes widen and she shrinks away from me. "Okay. Gosh, I never know what's happening around here."

"I mean it."

"*Okay*," she says again.

"Good." The three of us get out of the truck and walk in the back door, where Tony is whistling, Mom is adding fresh herbs to a giant pot of sauce, and Dad is nowhere to be found.

Nineteen

All afternoon and evening, the vision beats me over the head every chance they get, and it's exhausting. It's clear to me now that telling Sawyer was a good thing, but it wasn't enough. Apparently I have to get him to actually believe me too. And I'm guessing I have to get him to do something about it, which will be absolutely impossible. This is an evil game that is impossible to win.

And the thing is—that helpless, empty thing that makes me want to curl up in the corner and bawl my eyes out—it's that I know I can't make it happen. There's no way I can convince Sawyer or anybody that this crash will take place, and that nine people, including him, are going to die. And I think part of it is because I don't quite believe it myself. But if I don't believe this vision is destined to happen, then I have to believe I'm crazy.

This feels so much bigger than me, bigger than anything I can do, and I'm swallowed by it. Just thinking about facing Sawyer again, knowing he won't ever believe me, knowing if he mentions my weirdness to anyone it will ruin any reputation I have left, knowing that his family could so easily do something drastic that will make my father crack, just like my grandfather did, and knowing we could lose everything, scares the hell out of me.

I don't know what to do.

And for the first time, I think about real depression, the disease, and what that must feel like. I mean, my grandfather killed himself—he had a wife and kids and grandkids, and a business that he loved, and he just ended it all. Those good things in his life weren't enough for him. They couldn't stop his disease. To him, things seemed to crumble when Fortuno Angotti flourished. Only they didn't fall apart, they just stayed the same. And I guess that felt like failure to my grandfather. His insides, his brain, couldn't take it.

I heard my aunt Mary say once that my grandfather was a selfish person, hurting people like that, and I thought she was right. I've thought that about my dad, too. Lots of times.

But I don't know about that anymore. Everything about this, about mental illness, is so complicated. I just don't know.

The rest of the week, I am a zombie. I do what I need to do to get through the day. Talk if I have to. Get my homework done, not really caring if I do it right, seeing crash after crash after crash like I'm stuck in one minute that keeps repeating. On slow nights I send Rowan upstairs and work alone, keeping my mind occupied as best I can. Because I don't want to think about anything. I try to ignore the vision like I'd ignore a bug splat on the windshield. And I fail. It buzzes between my ears and crawls under my skin and coats the insides of my eyelids. The days blur together and soon it's another weekend. I ignore Trey's quizzical glances and Rowan's concerned looks and questions. I know I need to do something.

Maybe my grandfather knew that too. But he couldn't.
My father can't.
And I can't.

One morning I wake up to Rowan's alarm and stare at the wall. And it all becomes real. Nine real, human people, people with families and friends and jobs to do, will all die. And I am helpless, and I will never be the same again, and it doesn't matter that I actually told Sawyer what to expect, because if he doesn't believe me I'll still feel like it's my fault. The weight of this responsibility is so heavy, so crushing, I can't move.

"I'm sick," I tell Rowan when she stumbles out of bed. "Tell Trey he needs to get you to school today."

"What's wrong?"

I just close my eyes and moan. "Everything."

"You need me to get Mom?"

"No, don't wake her up. I'm okay, just sick."

I hear Rowan hesitating at the door. "I'll leave her a note to call in to school for you."

"Thanks," I say.

She closes the door.

Trey comes in a few minutes later. "Hey," he whispers.

I pretend to be asleep. There's a rattle of keys sliding off my dresser, and then he's gone.

Later, when my mom peeks her head in, I ignore her, too. Soon I hear Dad lumbering down the hallway, which means he actually got out of bed today.

I've taken his sickness from him. What a thing to pass down to the next generation.

All day, the wall is my only friend. If I don't look at the window, it's a day with few visions.

Still, the scene rolls through my brain regularly, and I

can't make it go away—the more I try, the more often the vision appears. I don't want to tell anyone—not a soul—but I admit to myself that I will need a doctor soon. And on the off chance that I'm not already insane, this vision will push me there. I think about what it'll be like to be in a hospital for people like that . . . people like me, I guess I should say. A hot tear slides from the corner of my eye into my hair. The thought of a crazy roommate scares me, like, a lot. The thought of having to take drugs that make me feel weird, of strange doctors asking me questions about the vision, of my mother with her overly cheerful face coming by to see me and pretending everything's just fine . . . I can't take it, I really can't.

Back when I was in first grade, when my father went crazy with the hoarding and the depression, he was in the hospital for a few days. I visited him—only once, though. I can still remember the smell of that place. His roommate was a scary man with white hair and a red-splotched face. His eyes bulged, and the scariest thing to me was that he didn't have any teeth. He walked up and down the hallway muttering to himself, and I was so afraid of his gummy maw coming after me that I slammed the door to my dad's room when he was coming in, and screamed when my mom tried to take me out of there, past him. Trey was with us, and Aunt Mary, too. We must have closed the restaurant . . . I don't remember. It doesn't really matter.

I wonder what goes through my father's mind every day. If it's anything like this, well, I guess I feel sorry for him.

Around two in the afternoon, I hear a soft knock on the door. I want to ignore it, but for some reason I say, "Come in."

It's my father. I turn over in bed, hoping I look as sick on the outside as I feel on the inside. "Hi," I say.

He looks scruffy and tired, but he's wearing his chef jacket. He puts a plate of toast, complete with parsley garnish, on my bedside table and sets a glass of clear carbonated liquid next to it. "I thought you might be getting hungry," he says, his normally booming voice softened. "Did I wake you up?"

I shake my head and sit up. "Thanks."

He puts the back of his hand on my forehead like Mom always does, and holds it there for a few seconds. Then he pulls it away and says nothing.

"It's more of a stomach thing," I say.

He nods, and we both know I'm lying.

"Well," he says. He fidgets with his hands, his big thumbs bumbling around each other, and I realize I hardly even know him at all. I've lived with this man for almost seventeen years and all I know about him is that he's an embarrassment to me. It kind of leaves a gigantic hole in my heart.

I wonder what he thinks about. If he ever thinks about killing himself. He turns to go, and I almost call out after him to wait. I almost whisper, "Do you ever see visions?" But I don't say anything.

The reason I don't is that even if his answer is no, I can guess that he, out of anyone in the world, will know why I'm asking—because I must be experiencing them. Which would lead to my parents putting me Someplace Else. And right now, today, a partly cloudy February day just outside of Chicago, I cannot risk leaving this bed for anything. Not for any doctor, not for any vision.

Not for any boy.

Twenty

When Trey sneaks upstairs after the dinner rush, around nine, he doesn't ask for permission to come in. He sits on the bed and looks at me.

"So. What are you sick of?"

I smirk. "You."

He rolls his eyes. "Are you going to live, or what?"

And that question, that joke, makes me hesitate. It burns through me. *Am I?* I look up at him, and my chest feels so much fear it squeezes my heart, makes it throb faster and faster.

"It's not a difficult question," he says with a smile, but I can see him searching me, trying to get inside my brain. He's been giving me a lot of looks like that lately. He knows me too well.

"Yes," I decide, thinking of body bags in the snow. "I'll live."

He rests his elbows on his knees, thumbs on his forehead, holding it up, massaging it, maybe. He closes his eyes, like he needs to think. And then he takes an audible breath and says, "I'm just gonna say this: You're not pregnant, are you?"

I almost laugh. And then my eyes get wide, because he's not laughing. "No, of course not. Is that what Dad thinks?"

"Yeah."

I let my head fall back on the pillow. "Jeez. I haven't even kissed anybody yet. I'm, like, the poster child for purity. I still have my freaking . . . my freaking . . ."

"Cherry?"

"No—"

"Hymen intact?"

I slug him. "Oh my God, shut *up*."

"Virginity?"

"Ugh! No! Well, yes, but—dammit, I can't think of the term. What's that thing girls used to wear in the olden days to keep the—just, never mind."

"Chastity belt?"

"Yeah. That. Sheesh. Joke gone horrendously wrong." I laugh, and it feels weird, like I haven't laughed in days.

Trey still holds a deadpan look. "So, to confirm:

You're not having an alien Antichrist baby from the seed of Angotti."

"Ah, no. Correct, I mean. Gross terminology threw me off."

"I will deliver the news thusly."

I stare at him. "Did he send you up here to ask me that?"

"No," Trey says, shifting his weight and relaxing on the bed. "I just read it in the worry lines on his forehead and figured I'd find out sooner rather than later, because I was wondering too."

"You?" I say, incredulous. "I am completely befuzzled by that. Don't you think I'd tell you if I managed to get close enough to Hottie Angotti to get pregnant?"

He shrugs and picks my cell phone up off the dresser. "You don't seem to tell me much at all lately," he says. He starts playing with it, pushing things on the screen.

I narrow my eyes and he turns so I can't see. "What are you doing? Searching my contacts or something?" I reach for the phone and he pulls it away. "Hey!"

"Calm it down, Demarco. I'm just playing Angry Bunnies."

"Oh." I struggle to sit up. I can feel my hair is all matted on one side. "Really? Or are you just saying that?"

"Yes, really. So what's going on with you?" he says, his eyes on the game, but I don't think he's actually playing it. "You're acting extremely weird these days."

At his words, memories of the vision pop into my mind again. I let my head bump against the wall, and I close my eyes. Like a rain cloud, all the dread, the helplessness, the fear, rush over me again, a waterfall of hurt, and I start to drown in it. A sigh escapes me, and then another, and another, until the sighs admit they are sobs and the bed starts to quiver.

"Aw, dang it, Jules," Trey says. "Come 'ere, then." Trey tugs on my arm; I bury my face in his shoulder and the tears come pouring out, a flood of them, and I can't stop it.

This is what I tell him through the sobs:

I am afraid of my life.

I am afraid of turning into Dad.

And, sometimes, I see things that aren't there.

He doesn't freak out, thankfully. But he's seriously concerned.

"What kind of things?"

"I don't know. . . ."

"Well, like giant spiders, or clowns, or imaginary friends, or ghosts, or what?"

I suck in a breath and let it out, beginning to regret the last five minutes with all my heart. I shouldn't have told him. "Like . . . a crash."

"You see car crashes that don't actually happen?" He

sits up straight, forehead wrinkled in alarm. "What, so you're crossing the street, and boom, there's a crash, metal crunching, people getting mangled and all of that, right in front of you?"

"No, not an actual crash. Just, like, a movie version of it. It's not physically happening in the street, I just see . . . pictures. Like a film. Like, everywhere."

"And you're aware . . . I mean—" He stares hard at my phone now, and I know what he's asking.

"Yes," I say, my voice turning clinical. "I'm cognizant of the fact that this is not normal, yet I can't stop it."

He blinks. "I don't get it."

"Me neither."

Trey stares at me for a long moment and puts my phone on my bedside table. "Kiddo, I know you don't want to hear this, but I really—"

"No."

"Jules, I mean it—"

"No, Trey," I say again, firmer this time.

"I think," he says even more firmly, "we should tell Mom."

"No!" I say. "No! Please—I trusted you. And we can't tell her. No way. She'll . . ." I imagine all the things she'll do, unable to decide which is the worst. Freak out. Pretend everything is fanfreakingtastic. Or worst of all, tell Dad. "Ugh," I say, sliding down in the bed, turning to face the wall, and pulling the covers over my head. And then I say softly, "She'll put me in the hospital, Trey. Like Dad."

At first, I can't tell if he hears me. He doesn't deny it. He doesn't answer at all. And then, once time begins again, he sighs deeply, and I feel his hand squeeze my shoulder. "Okay," he says. "We'll think about it. Talk it through, figure out what to do. All right? Let me know if it gets worse."

I close my eyes and let out a breath of relief. "Yeah."

Twenty-One

All night I dream about it—the crash, the explosion, the nine body bags in the snow, the fire. Sawyer's dead face. But in my dreams the events happen in random order. At the end, the body bags stand up and dance around in the snowy, fiery night, as if they are ghosts trying to get out of their containments. Sawyer's eyes fly open and he cries out to me for help, but I just walk away, going into a hospital that magically appears next door. Doctors take me by the hands and I begin to shrink. As I get smaller they swing me like a little kid down the hallway, and then they let go and I soar into a jail-like cell with bars on the doors. The doors clank shut. I hear someone muttering and cackling, and when I look up, a toothless, red-faced scary guy is locked in my cell with me.

I wake up kicking and sweating. Rowan is standing next to my bed saying my name.

I stare at her. It takes me a second to remember where I am. "Oh," I say, breathing hard. "Hey."

"Are you okay?"

I swallow, my throat totally dry, and then nod. "Yeah. Bad dream."

"Oh," she says. "Well, you were kind of moaning, or crying or something." She goes back to her bed and sits on the edge of it, facing me.

"I was?" My brain is a cotton ball.

She nods in the dark. "You kept saying, '*Listen* to me!'"

I unwind my leg from the bedsheet. "Huh." The nightmare is already starting to fade and the jagged pieces of it aren't fitting together anymore. "Did I say anything else?"

"Nothing that I could figure out. Are you still sick?"

I continue to untangle myself from my blankets and ponder the question. When I think about going to school, about seeing Sawyer, about the vision everywhere, my stomach churns and I feel like throwing up. "Yeah," I decide. "I'm still sick."

It's light in the room when I wake again, and I feel refreshed, like I've slept a hundred years. Rowan is gone, the house is quiet, and the first doughy smells of the day are wafting up from below. I sit up and check the clock. It's almost eleven, and I'm starving. My head feels . . . I don't know. Less heavy or something. I can't really identify the feeling, but it's a kind of restlessness. Like my feet are tired of being in this bed. My legs won't stay still.

I get up and stretch, testing my muscles, and tentatively think about the vision, bracing myself for that overwhelming fear to take over, but it doesn't. The fear is still there, all right, but it's . . . I don't know. More manageable. Softer, maybe. The vision appears on the window, as it has been doing lately, but today it is less in-your-face. It stays in the background, and I can actually think around it. I don't even know if that makes sense, but that's how it feels.

I pad softly to the kitchen and toast a bagel in the quiet. It's so strange to be the only one up here. So nice. I take my breakfast to the chair in the living room and tuck my toes up under my nightgown. I sit there and soak in the sounds of the street below—a garbage truck, an occasional honk of a horn, an exuberant Italian greeting a friend now and then.

I think about the snowplow again and close my eyes to ward off the panic, but the panic doesn't come, only a controllable fear, one that I can handle. I marvel at myself, wondering where the calm came from. Maybe it was the twelve hours of sleep, or crying it out with Trey last night, or the nightmare working something out for me in my subconscious, like Mr. Polselli talked about once in a section on dreams. But as I sit here, I think maybe it's something else. Maybe it's coming from the same source that brought me this vision in the first place. Maybe it's telling me that it's not quite as futile as it seems, and it's trying to give me directions now and then if I would only listen.

I think about that for a long time.

Later, I take a rare long shower. With one bathroom for five people, there's hardly ever enough time or hot water for something so luxurious. But today I stand here, eyes closed, letting the water beat down and the steam float over my skin and into my lungs. I wash my body, scrub the grease out of my hair, and smooth conditioner through it. At one point, thinking about the conversation yesterday with Trey, about how he and Dad thought I was pregnant, I just shake my head and almost laugh.

But then my mind wanders to Sawyer. To sixth grade, and to my Sawyer pillow, and my dreams of kissing him. The water burrows down on my lips, my neck. My collarbone. I turn my hips slowly side to side, and suddenly I can feel every thread of water moving over my skin, making it come alive.

I don't really understand why a shower feels so good sometimes, and other times it's just a shower, but I guess I needed it to feel good today, and it does. I let out a heavy sigh, and my fingers, down at my sides, travel lightly against the current, up my thighs and over my hips, my stomach, to my breasts, and back down. When the water starts to turn cool, urgent heat keeps me warm from the inside. My head bows, streams of water pouring off my hair. I squeeze my knees shut, hands clenched between my thighs, and I just crouch there, feeling so much life and love and risk and terror pulsing around me, inside me, that I don't know what to do with the overwhelming all-ness of it.

A painful longing takes over my skin and bones, and I move to let the water splash on my face and chest once again. It exhilarates me more and more the colder it grows, until it's shocking enough to halt and restart my breath a dozen times, and I'm almost too cold to turn it off.

I think it shocked me into reality or something. I stand in the tub for a minute, dripping, not shivering, my cold skin glowing from the adrenaline and utter grief inside. I think about how weird it is that loving someone just makes everything hurt so much more. But I guess it's that pain that means you're alive, and love and pain are so . . . so twisty. I wonder if love would feel as good if there wasn't any pain. I don't think it could. So I guess that's kind of what makes life worth living.

It's so bizarre, but I feel like I grew up in this one moment.

Before my heart rate slows and my skin is dry, everything becomes so clear to me. And despite the grimness of
my task, I can't believe I've let so much stand in the way of
this thing I have been mysteriously tasked to do.

Twenty-Two

With Mom and Dad downstairs in the restaurant and Trey and Rowan at school, I have the whole apartment to myself. I flip on the ancient computer and then rummage around for a sandwich, waiting impatiently for the weather forecast to load. Out the window, the sun shines, unless you look a little farther down the road, where in a storefront window, a crash and an explosion in a snowstorm is happening right . . . now.

The page loads and, surprise, in place of each little weather icon is a picture of an explosion. Nice touch, weird brain. At least the forecast description is still there. As of this moment, there's only a 10 percent chance of snow showers tonight. A 20 percent chance tomorrow, and a 40 percent chance Friday, and then it looks like there might be a storm coming on the weekend. I study it, and it's a bit of a relief that the next couple days look reasonably clear.

"Okay," I mutter, feeling hopeful. "Okay. We most likely have some time to work with here." But it would be really freaking nice if I could narrow down the date of this crash. That one thing would make this huge uncertainty more manageable, and it would make it easier to convince Sawyer . . .

"Oh, hell," I say. "What am I thinking?" Convincing Sawyer will be one of the hardest things I've ever done in my life. None of this will be easy. Not one thing about this will be easy at all. And I'm almost certain I'll fail.

Nine body bags in the snow.

Before I can send myself back to the overwhelming abyss of hopelessness, I grip the desk and grit my teeth and take a deep breath, letting it out slowly. "Hang on, Demarco. Just calm it down and hang on."

First things first. I have two hours with the TV to myself, and by the time it's over, I will know every detail of that scene backward and forward and inside out.

I flip on the TV and I don't even have to search for it. It plays on a loop. I watch it like that for several minutes just to get back into the timing of the events. Obviously the scenes are not one continuous shot, but where exactly are the breaks? I grab my notebook and take notes about my observations:

Scene 1: The snowplow is coming down Cottonwood Street behind Angotti's. My view is approximately from the parking lot near the Angotti's building. While it's dark, it's only a little hard to see the truck, because the streetlights are on. It seems to me that the truck is going way too fast for a mostly residential neighborhood. It's not going very straight. It crosses to the wrong side of the road and angles toward the back parking lot of Angotti's. It hits the curb, goes over a pile of snow, and bounces roughly. That's where the scene breaks.

As I watch, I realize a couple of things. First, how can the snowplow hop the curb like that if the plow is down? I rewind and watch again in the earliest second of the scene, and I can see in the dark that the plow is not actually down. Yet the street is pretty freshly cleared.

Scene 2: It appears that this scene immediately follows scene 1, but the viewpoint is different. I see the snowplow from the back this time, as if I'm standing in the rear of the parking lot, and the plow is still rocking after jumping the curb and snow pile. It has a clear path to the restaurant, which is now in sight, and I can see people in the window. The snowplow doesn't slow down at all. It hits the building, and the people inside never even appear to see it coming until that last second. Some glass flies before I see fire and the rest of the place exploding. Then smoke and pieces of brick and glass falling all around. That's the end of scene 2.

As I watch this scene over and over, I take note of the height of the snow piles in the parking lot—there's been a decent amount of snow plowed along the parking lot edges, and it's almost all white, not too dirty, which makes me think it's quite fresh. I stare at the pile height and try to find something physical I can compare it to. I crawl up close to the TV and look hard. There's a No Parking sign on that side of the road. The snow comes about a third of the way up, I guess, but it's hard to tell. On the opposite side of the street I see the top of a fire hydrant sticking out. I draw a picture of it in my notebook, showing where the snow line is. I bite my lip in anticipation, feeling the tiniest bit of hope that I'll be able to narrow down the day this happens by taking a daily drive up that street and seeing where the snow level is.

Scene 3: It's a simple scene. My viewpoint this time is from the rubble, it seems. There are nine body bags in the snow. They are laid out on the far edge of the parking lot, along the avenue parallel to Cottonwood Street. There's a band of yellow police tape attached to the maple trees that line the road on that side. There are people in stride and standing about, but their heads and shoulders are all cut from the scene, which centers on the bags. There is a wisp of smoke, and while I don't see any emergency vehicles in this shot, the snow has a red glow to it in one spot, and blue in another, which makes me think lights are probably on.

Vehicles are still there. Then the final frame—a close-up of the three bags on the right. The one on the end is open, and Sawyer's dead face is visible.

It stops me cold, even though I've seen it at least a thousand times by now. There's something about today, about the good night's sleep and the shower and the personal pep talk and the notebook, writing down details, that finally makes this seem very real. "This is happening," I say, staring at the screen, and for the first time I'm deeply convinced. It's not a joke. It's not a mind game. And what's more, I'm starting to think I'm not insane—or I'm caring less about my own personal crap and how this crash will affect *me*. "This is really going to happen, Demarco. You're going to have to do something."

Of course, if you ask any psych student, they'll say that's the first sign you're insane—that you think you aren't. There's no real win in the insanity department. And I realize, as I sit here staring at Sawyer's closed eyes, that even on the totally off chance I can get Sawyer out of that building at exactly the right time to save him, it won't matter much, because he'll be so traumatized about losing everything else.

And everyone else.

Who else is in those body bags?

The enormity of the task overwhelms me again, and I can feel my gut begin to twist. It makes me want to crawl back into bed and hide, pretend this isn't happening. Instead, I crouch down on the living room floor, among the hoarded junk, and wrap my arms around my knees, rocking back and forth a little, thinking. Thinking it all through.

Wondering if there's a way I could shut the whole restaurant down for one night so the plow crashes into a vacant building. Maybe I could somehow break the big window or cut the electricity. But I know that wouldn't keep the family from being in the restaurant—that's exactly where they'd all flock to so they could figure out how to fix things. So there goes that idea.

But then a brand-new wonder hits me.

Do the body bags in the snow mean it's inevitable? Will those nine people die no matter what I do or don't do? Is it really their time to go, or can death be prevented? I don't know.

I just don't know.

Twenty-Three

I'm staring at Sawyer's dead face for the zillionth time when I hear people coming up the steps. Rowan and Trey jostle each other in the tight entrance, taking winter gear off. I push play and wonder what TV show I'm actually watching—what they'll see and hear. To me, the crash scenes loop as usual with no sound. I guess this means I won't get to watch anything again until this is all over.

Rowan and Trey come in and see me. Rowan glances at the TV and frowns. "You must be very sick to watch that crap," she says. "Sheesh. Turn it down. The customers will hear."

I shrug. Curious, but too lazy to try and figure it out, I turn the TV off. "I'm feeling a little better."

"Good," Trey says. He has a new, concerned look in his eyes, and he's trying not to be obvious about monitoring me. I wonder what he's thinking. I smile at him like we share a secret, and I think that reassures him.

"So, school tomorrow, maybe?" he asks.

"Maybe."

"Hey, are you, like, pregnant or something?" Rowan says out of the blue.

"Oh my gosh," I say, giving Trey a look. "Where would you possibly get that idea?"

"I heard Mom and Dad whispering last night."

"Great. Can one of you please hurry up and assure them that I am not pregnant? I have never even kissed a boy." I hesitate. "No, don't tell them that. Mom'll tell everybody who walks in the door."

"You don't have to be kissed to get pregnant," Rowan says. She pulls a piece of gum out of her backpack and shoves it in her mouth.

"I'm aware of the process, thank you," I say.

Trey laughs. "Apparently, so is Rowan."

Rowan blushes furiously. "Shut up."

Trey pushes her shoulder and she pretends to fall over. "I'm heading down in a minute," he says to me. "I'll make sure everybody in the restaurant knows you are not pregnant."

"This is all really embarrassing, you know," I say. Trey

leaves and I call out after him, "How is it that everyone in my family thinks I'm out having sex? I don't ever leave this place. There's no time to get pregnant around here!" I look at Rowan.

She's watching me, grinning.

"Go," I say. I point to the door. "Don't you have to work or something?"

"Somebody around here has to. Lazy butt."

"Go!"

She leaves to change clothes, and I sit here again to stew over what to do. I look outside in the waning afternoon light on a cold, snowless day and again feel relieved that I've got a bit of time on my hands to work with.

I'm just not sure how to tackle the next thing on my list—convincing Sawyer that something bad is going to happen, and watching him look at me like I'm nuts, all while avoiding threats from his father that could make my father kill himself.

This is where the whole love-and-pain thing comes in, right here. But I'm newly determined, and I can't let my heart stop me from totally alienating the boy I love . . . or soon all I'll be loving will be the memory of him.

Before Rowan goes down to the restaurant, she peeks into the living room again, and hesitates. "Hey, Jules?" she says in an earnest voice.

"What's up?" I say. I pat the arm of my chair, which

is the only place she can sit. She comes over and perches next to me, and I put my arm around her waist like when we were younger. "You okay?"

She nods. "I guess. I just . . ." She looks at me. "What do you think about long-distance relationships?"

I stare at her and skip over the formalities. "What? Why? With who?"

"I don't know, just in general—"

"Who?" I demand.

"A guy."

"How did you meet this guy who doesn't live near us?" I know my voice is getting loud, but I have a weird feeling. "Not on the Internet or anything, right?"

She scowls at me. "Yeah, his online username is ChildPredator77. I sent him pictures of my naked budding bazooms and he wants to meet me behind the Dumpster at Pete's Liquor to give me candy. Jeez, Jules! Of course not. I'm not stupid."

I sigh in relief. "Okay. Wow. Sorry. Of course you're not stupid. So how . . . ?"

"Soccer camp during fall break."

"Oh." I search my memory, trying to recall if she ever talked about a boy. "Have you been in contact with . . . wait, what's his name?"

"Charlie. Yeah. We video chat during second hour almost every day."

I blink.

"I have study hall in the library. He's sort of home-schooled. I met his parents when they picked him up."

My lips part but I can't think of anything to say.

She turns to look at me. "They've invited me to come for spring break."

Silence.

"They offered to pay for my ticket, but that felt weird so I'm saving up my tips to go. They live in New York." She snaps her fingers in my face. "Hello? Any reaction at all would be appreciated."

I shake my head, dumbfounded. "But . . . a week or two ago you said you didn't have a boyfriend."

"It wasn't official yet then. We've been taking it slow."

"New York? Really?"

She nods. "So? What do you think?"

I say the first thing that comes to mind. "You're fifteen. There's no way Mom and Dad will let you."

Rowan rolls her eyes to the ceiling. "Besides that."

"Have you two . . . did you . . . ," I stammer. "Um . . ."

"We held hands and kissed once. That's all."

"That's all," I echo, lost in melancholy thoughts. And then I catch myself and shoot her the best smile I can fake. "I'm really happy for you, Ro."

"And the long-distance thing?"

I shrug. "I think if anybody can make it work, it's you."

She grins and hops off the chair arm. "Thanks, Jules. I was hoping you'd say that. I really like him." She reaches down and hugs me, then hurries to the restaurant, leaving me alone to dwell in the chair as dusk settles over the hoards.

But there's no time to feel sorry for myself. I mean, big whoop—my younger sister likes a boy and she's making it work. Do I care that she kissed somebody before me? Hell no. Hell no I don't. It's not a contest. Besides, I have a lot of other, more important crap to think about right now.

Around seven, when I know everyone will be busy, I grab the meatball truck keys from Trey's room and sneak out.

It takes me a little less than five minutes to get to Angotti's. I park on the next block so they can't see my truck. As I walk I pull my collar up and my hat down to my eyebrows and wrap my scarf around my face.

When I reach their enormous back parking lot, I do a snow-level check. There's definitely a little snow piled up along the road, but it's nowhere near a third of the way up the No Parking sign or the top of the hydrant across the street. One good snow could change all that, but it'd have to be a decent storm, I'd say.

I walk slowly up the sidewalk, studying Angotti's from the back, trying to pretend that I'm just taking a walk on this cold evening in case any of the family or employees pop out the back door to take out trash. I get a decent look into the dining room window. People sit in the booths there now, enjoying pizza and beer. I look for Sawyer but he's not in the dining room, as far as I can tell.

As I get closer, I try to remember all the things I wrote in my notebook and curse myself for forgetting to bring it with me. I stop for a moment, push my hat back, and give myself more room to breathe around the scarf, and look inside as much as I can, trying to figure out the exact layout. I should have looked a few days ago when I was inside, but I'd had other things on my mind and didn't think of it then. And something seems off. I can't place it, but it doesn't look exactly the same as the scene. I can't tell what it is. I take a few steps closer, trying to stay in the shadows so that people inside won't notice me. I look all around the dining room, from the service station to the giant forks and knives on the walls to the antique clock with ivy all around to the arrangement of the tables. Maybe that's what's off—the tables aren't quite in the same spots as in the scene I keep seeing. I narrow my eyes. But I still can't place it.

My teeth start chattering, but I weave my way between a few cars in the lot, trying to get a closer look at the building itself. The back door flies open and I spin around, pretending to walk toward a car. I glance over my shoulder, and it's a short-haired blond girl with heavy eye makeup carrying a trash bag. She props the door open with her foot and picks up a second bag, maneuvering them through the opening.

"The fifteenth," she's saying to someone in the kitchen. "No, I can totally work Saturday. Not going to the dance. I need the *fifteenth* off." She lets the door close and walks over to the Dumpster, hoists the bags inside, then wipes her hands on her pants and pulls a pack of cigarettes out of her coat pocket. She flips one out and lights it, taking a deep drag.

I crouch behind a car, stuck here until she goes back in, unless I want to risk her seeing me appearing out of nowhere and walking away. A car pulls into the parking lot and I turn to look at it, its lights bouncing on me for a few seconds.

It would have been better if I hadn't done that.

It's Sawyer's mother. She takes one alarmed look at me, then hits the gas and pulls up to the back door of the restaurant.

I bite my lip, not sure what to do. In a panic, I make a run for it, down the sidewalk into the neighborhood. "Shit!" I say when I'm far enough away. I keep running, turning the corner, around the block to my meatball truck. "Shit, shit, shit." And then I'm speeding home as fast as I can so I can get back upstairs, get into my pajamas, and establish my alibi.

Thoughts fly through my head. Did I leave any finger-prints anywhere? No, I was wearing gloves the whole time. But the meatball truck's engine will be warm. The restraining order police will check that when they come after me, and they'll know I'm lying. Should I just tell the truth? What's my dad going to do? I park the truck and throw snow on the hood to make it look like it's been sitting there all day, which I know is stupid, but I'm not thinking straight, and then I fly up the stairs, hoping, pleading, that there's no one up there waiting to catch me.

The apartment is empty.

Just as I left it.

I breathe a sigh of relief and hang up my winter things.

Five minutes later, the phone rings.

Twenty-Four

I stare at the phone, and then make a mad dash to check the caller ID. It's a cell number, no name. The area code is local. And I don't know what to do. If it's Mr. Angotti, I'll die. But it's probably a telemarketer. But what if it's not? If it's Mr. Angotti, I don't want him to leave a message . . . or worse, try the restaurant line and get my dad.

That decides it. I lunge for the phone and pick it up, forcing myself to control my voice.

"Hello?" I say, like my mother would say.

There is a momentary silence on the other end, and I think it must be a telemarketer after all.

And then, in a puzzled voice, "Jules?"

I die inside. "Yes?" I say, my voice filled with air,

not just because of the exertion of lunging halfway across a room.

"It's Sawyer. Look, what the heck are you doing?"

Now I'm silent. And guilty. But I'm going to fake it. "What are you talking about?"

"My mother saw you."

"Saw me where?"

"In the parking lot. Tonight. Come on."

I hesitate. "Dude, I've been home sick for two days."

"I know that. Doesn't mean you weren't out in our parking lot twenty minutes ago."

He knows that, he said. He noticed I was sick. I feel a surge of confidence bordering on recklessness. "You're sounding a little paranoid, Sawyer. Why, exactly, would I be in your parking lot in the freezing cold when I'm sick?"

"You tell me."

"This is an extremely weird conversation."

He pauses, and I think I hear a soft laugh. "Yeah. Pretty weird." His voice goes back to normal. "So you really weren't there?"

I sigh. "Oh, Sawyer," I say, and my voice sounds all throaty—almost sexy, which is, um, new for me. I blink at my reflection in the computer screen.

Now he laughs sheepishly. "Okay, so my mom's the paranoid one. Sorry about that."

"Where are you?"

"Ahh," he says, and I wonder if he's not sure, or if he's afraid to tell me. "I'm . . . out. For the moment."

"Don't worry, I'm not going to stalk you. Look, since I've got you on the phone," I say carefully, "I wonder if you've given any more thought to the little thing I told you last Sunday. You know, the thing where there's going to be a crash, and I'm kind of trying to save your life, and you think I'm insane. Because, to be honest, I could really use your help."

"Jules, no," he says, and I can hear a hint of annoyance in his voice. "I mean, yes, I thought about it, and no, I'm no longer thinking about it, and it's really weird and creepy, and I was hoping you'd have moved past it too. And maybe we could pretend it didn't happen."

I nod, phone plastered to my ear. "Yeah, that's what I figured. Okay. Well." Suddenly I get all choked up, because it's all so newly real to me, and it's so weirdly fake to him, and I can't stop the emotion, because I'm just . . . mired in this. This thing is running my entire life, but it's just a tiny blip in his. Until one day, *bam!* And then it's over for him. None of this is fair in any way.

But I'm determined not to let him die without me making a complete fool of myself in an effort to stop it. I close my eyes. "Well," I say again, my voice quavering, "I just want you to know that whether you help me or not, that's okay. I understand. And I'm still going to, ah"—my voice turns to gravel—"do whatever I can to . . ." I can't say it.

He's silent, and I wonder if he hung up.

I take a breath. "Are you still there?" I ask.

"Yeah," he says.

"Oh."

There's a pause.

"Whatever you can to . . . what?" he says.

"Um . . ." I close my eyes. And I figure he's going to die, so why not? "Save you. Yeah."

"Jules," he says again. "You're nuts."

"Sawyer," I reply, and now I'm pissed because he actually said it to my face, or to my ear or whatever. "I'm not nuts. I don't know what I am, but I'm not nuts. I'm not normally weird, even though this particular episode in our lifelong soap opera seems that way. But I do—I—I do—I care about you. And I'm going to save your life, and you probably won't even know it, or believe me afterward, either." I take a breath. "But I can't *not* do it. So I don't care if your father puts out a restraining order on me, or your grandfather breaks my father's heart after he already did my grandfather in, or whatever. You just do whatever you Angottis have to do to feel superior to the Demarcos until the end of time—that's just, you know, fine with me, and that's, like, capitalism and shit. But goddammit, Sawyer, despite all that, I'm going to save your fucking life anyway, because I love you, and one day you'd better fucking appreciate it."

I wait, shocked at myself.

After a long pause, he says, "Wow."

"Yeah? So?"

"So basically, what you're saying is, my mother actually did see you in the parking lot tonight."

My eyes spring open, and before I can think, I yell, "Ugh! My God! You are such a jerk!" And I slam down the phone in disgust.

Then I realize that slamming it didn't actually hang it up, so I pick it up again and jab the off button really, really stinking hard, and bang the phone down into its cradle again.

I stare at the desk, and all I can do is shake my head at myself. "You? Are bumblefucking nuts, Demarco."

Five reasons why I, Jules Demarco, am nuts:
1. I just screamed at the boy I love
2. I just told the boy I love that I love him.
   Ugh.
3. I pretty much admitted that I was lurking in
   his parking lot
4. And tried to make his mother look paranoid
5. Then there's that vision thing

You know, though, there's something really energizing, or, no, that's not even the right word—empowering, I suppose one of those Dr. Phil speaker types would say—about screaming at someone, and almost not caring what they think anymore. Because what's happening here is so much bigger than all of that. After nine years of loving Sawyer Angotti, and worrying about everything I say and do in or near his presence or in the presence of anyone who knows him, and being mad and embarrassed at myself repeatedly for laughing too loud, or saying something that wasn't *good* enough for his ears to hear, I feel pretty freaking awesome.

Awesome enough to think about putting a big sign on my head that says, "Yeah, I love you. So the hell what?"

Before I head to bed, I go back to the phone and grab Sawyer's cell number from the caller ID, enter it into my cell phone contacts, and erase the number from caller ID memory.

Because I just might need it one day.

Twenty-Five

I catch the scenes on TV while waiting for Rowan to finish up in the bathroom. And they're everywhere I go. I have to be careful driving now—all the road signs are stills of the explosion or of Sawyer's face, so I either have to recognize the sign by shape or go by memory of where stop signs are, and remember what the speed limit is through residential areas. The trip from home to school is an easy one, but this could be a problem the next time I do deliveries.

However, I don't spend a lot of time thinking about road signs. I don't even bother to look at Sawyer once I get to school, as much as it pains me. I don't think all that much about what people might be saying about me behind my back, and to my own amazement, I care even less. All day at school my mind is occupied with details. What am I missing? How can I figure it out? Even brief thoughts of Rowan vid chatting with her boyfriend during second hour don't sway my focus.

And then, in the middle of fifth period, when I'm going over the details of last night's visit to the parking lot, what I need to do hits me like a freight train.

Between classes I text to Trey and Rowan: "Rowan, go home with Trey. Have to stop at library for stupid research paper." I almost run over my former friend Roxie and her BFF Sarah, who are standing in the middle of the hallway as I type. My shoulder brushes Roxie's armload of pink and red construction paper and sends it sliding across the floor in all directions.

"Watch it, freak!" she says.

I almost apologize. I almost help her pick it all up and let her call me a freak and just take it, take it, take it—that's the Demarco way. But instead I look at her, and at Sarah, and back at Roxie again. "That's *insane* freak," I say. "Get it right." And I keep walking.

After school I high-five Trey and head out the door, right past Sawyer and his group of friends, including Roxie. He raises an eyebrow at me, and I shrug. Yeah, I love you. Yeah, I was in your stupid parking lot. So the hell what?

That stomach flip is still there, big-time. But my sudden decision to be the insane freak at school makes me feel like a totally different person—like nobody can touch me, because I'm on my own.

Oh yeah, baby. I'm on my own.

At the library I make a little wish as I head to the computers. I don't know if this is going to work, but I'm going to try. I find a vacant station in the corner, away from others, and sit down. I pull up an entertainment website and click on the first TV video I see—some reality show called *Skinny Wallets, Fat Love*. It doesn't matter what it is. The video loads a hundred times faster than it would at home, and I push play.

"Nice," I mutter as the all-too-familiar scenes play out. I maximize it and expertly hit pause at just the right place, the frame where we're looking into Angotti's dining room. I squint, trying to see past the snowflakes, past the people in the window, to the interior wall, where the giant antique clock hangs.

I take a screenshot and zoom in, hoping I can still make out the whole pixilated mess.

And there it is—the clue I've been searching for.

It's the giant clock on the wall, and its hands rest on four minutes past seven. And since Angotti's isn't open for breakfast, it's definitely got to be in the evening.

"7:04 p.m.," I whisper. I stare harder, trying to make out the second hand, but it's no use. The exact second won't be known, but getting it down to the minute is pretty awesome.

"Jules, you are a genius," I whisper. "Now you just need to synchronize."

A voice startles me back to the present. "Yo, insane freak. Talking to yourself?" It's BFF Sarah, trying to sound tough, sitting down at the computer two seats away. She takes out a notebook.

I frown. "What do you want?"

"You messed up our V-Day Dance decorations."

"Maybe you shouldn't be standing in the middle of a crowded hallway with them, then." Where I'd normally be scared, I am now bold. I look at her and wait for her response.

She wavers just slightly. "You're pissed because nobody ever invites you. That's why you did it."

I glance back at my screen and minimize it, then look back to her. "Invites me to what?"

"Anything. Homecoming. Winter Ball. Valentine's Dance."

I sigh and wonder if she's feeling *empowered* today too. If she is, it's not working. I lean toward her. "Did you come here to harass me?"

She doesn't respond, probably because she's so dumb she doesn't have an answer. She pulls out some papers and ignores me.

I go back to studying my screenshot.

But she's not done. A minute later, she says, "Is that what made you insane, freak? You're in love with Sawyer Angotti, but he never asks you to anything, and now you've lost your marbles. It is, isn't it." It's not a question.

My neck grows warm. There's only one way she could have found out I told Sawyer I love him. Unless she's just digging at me. That's probably more likely. I stare at my computer screen and say nothing, heeding the inner instinct to brace myself for more.

"But you can't help being insane, can you," Sarah says in a pitying voice. "Your family and all."

I close my eyes and grip my chair arms. In my mind, I decimate her. I scream, I kick, I hurt her on the outside for what she just did to my insides. I take a measured breath, and then I open my eyes and turn slowly toward her, covering my teeth with my lips and imitating that scary, gummy man from the hospital when Dad was there. In a harsh voice, I whisper, "Do you want to find out how crazy I really am?"

Twenty-Six

It was pretty awesome seeing Sarah react to that, I have to admit. She pushed her chair back with a loud scrape and her eyes went wide, her mouth open, her wad of gum just sitting there, tempted to roll out. And then she pulled her stuff together, called me a lunatic, and took off. I wonder if she got her assignment done. Tsk.

I spend an hour studying close-ups of each scene, landing again on the one quick shot of the dining room window. There's still something odd, but I can't figure it out. I spend a couple bucks to print out all the screen-shots, but when I go to pick them up off the printer, they're not there. There's just a stack of color shots of

Skinny Wallets, Fat Love. Now I really do look insane.

"Big sigh, Demarco," I mutter under my breath. "Maybe next time print just one and check it, hey?"

Once I get home, everybody's down in the restaurant already. So I start digging for a disguise.

I sort through the hoards and piles and boxes. Because I know that somewhere in here, there's a whole crap ton of Halloween costumes. And I definitely can't be recognized again—at least not right now.

After an hour, and just when I'm about to give up and get my butt to work, I find the mother lode in the far corner of the dining room, under a musty box of canning jars, which we keep in case we ever decide to fix the seventeen broken pressure cookers in the living room, which we'll do if we ever learn how to can things. It all makes sense, doesn't it? Especially since we have all this spare time to take up hobbies.

Anyway, right on top of the pile are some retro glasses and three wigs: Elvira, Marilyn Monroe, and a generic one with brown dreadlocks, or maybe it's Bob Marley, I'm not sure. I shake them, and only dust falls out—a good sign that even the mice are repulsed. A careful sniff of each doesn't kill me or even knock me flat, so I confiscate them, putting them into a plastic bag and shoving them under my bed.

•　　•　　•

Five useful things about living with a fairly clean hoarder:
1. If you look around long enough, you're bound to find something for a science project
2. There are endless opportunities for organizing if you have OCD
3. The potential for canning is good to great
4. It's easy to hide things in plain sight, like gnomes and bird cages an' shit
5. Survival rate is over one full year when zombies attack

When I walk downstairs and into the restaurant, Rowan and Trey are standing on chairs at the entryway to the dining room, both with rolls of masking tape on their wrists and strings of shiny heart cutouts around their necks.

I tie my apron around my waist and squint up at them. "Seriously? Do we really have to encourage it?"

"Sing it," Trey mutters. He slaps a circle of tape on the back of a red heart and sticks it to the trim work.

"Oh, come on," Rowan says. "It's a beautiful tradition. Mom found those heart-shaped pizza pans."

"Wasn't too beautiful for the martyred dude," Trey says.

"Heart-shaped pans. Like we need more crap," I mutter as the front door jingles and Dad walks in with two magazines and a newspaper. Trey snorts and Rowan's eyes bug out.

"Feeling better?" Dad asks me. He doesn't look quite so freaked out as he did the other day. I glance at Trey, who has a ribbon in his mouth. He nods once from his perch.

"Yeah, I guess it was just the flu or meningitis or black hairy tongue disease or something other than pregnancy."

Dad blushes and pretends he doesn't get it. "Take it easy tonight. You need to be ready for Saturday."

"I know." Mentally I calculate the date and day of the week—being sick always throws me off. I've been thinking it's Monday all day, but it's Thursday. No wonder everybody's hanging pink and red stuff everywhere. When Valentine's Day falls on the weekend, it's always out of control.

I get into the dining room to give Aunt Mary a hand as five o'clock rolls around and the early bird diners arrive, right on cue. The decorations are all up in here already. Trey and Rowan must have started right after school. They have them draped in a lovely, nontacky way across the picture windows. Both Rowan and Trey are pretty artistic, which is why they're hanging decorations and I'm serving. I get the drink orders for the first two tables by the windows while regretting being unable to print the pictures I wanted at the library.

When I'm setting down their drinks, a shiny, dangling heart turns on its twine and catches the light, sparkling. I fight off the twinge of longing inside. Maybe BFF Sarah is right, and I'm sad and pissed that nobody ever asks me to go to any dances. And that I'm almost seventeen and I still haven't had my first kiss. I stare at the heart for a second and then turn away before the patrons think I'm weird.

And then, halfway to the kitchen, it hits me. I stop, stand, and pivot to look at it once more as it catches the light. "Shit," I whisper. "Really?" I drop off my tray and run through the kitchen, past Tony and Dad, and out the back door, almost wiping out in my haste to get into the door to the apartment, and race up the stairs.

I flip on the TV and watch the scenes unfold, pause on the dining room window, and stare at it. Crawl up to the screen and stare harder. "Oh my dogs," I say. I turn the TV off, grab the spare delivery-car key, my coat, and the Marilyn wig, and fly back downstairs, outside, to the car, and take off, not even caring if anybody's watching me, or if anybody needs a pizza delivered. Because this can't wait.

Twenty-Seven

I pull into the parking lot of Angotti's as dusk turns to dark. On my head is the platinum-blond wig, and I'm trying hard not to think about there being any bugs in it. I have one directive—I need to get to approximately where I'd be standing if I had been recording the scene, about twenty or thirty feet from the building and slightly off to the side closer to the back door. I need to have that perspective. I turn the engine off and hop out, holding my wig on my head and using the car as cover.

In my vision, there are light fixtures in the window, hanging from the ceiling—I could see them through the window. I remember noticing they weren't there the first time I came here to look at everything, but that was because it was the night of the wedding, and I assumed the tables were all rearranged.

But they're still not there. Nothing's hanging in the window. People sit there eating, but the lights are either recessed or too high to be seen.

Or maybe they weren't lights at all.

Maybe they were decorations.

"Valentine's Day," I murmur, and the missing piece falls into place. "Snowstorm forecasted for this weekend. Those were decorations hanging down, not lights. Jeez." I shake my head. "This whole thing happens on Valentine's Day?" A surge of fear pulses through me. "Could the timing be any worse?"

As I stand there in the shadows, the back door to the kitchen swings open hard, slamming against the block wall and ringing out into the quiet night. It's Sawyer. "Let it go," he's saying to the bright beam of light that follows him. His voice is angry. "I'm telling you, don't engage with that son of a bitch. You're just enabling him."

The blond girl I saw the other night follows Sawyer out and slams the door shut. She stands on the step lighting a cigarette while Sawyer tosses broken-down cardboard boxes into the recycling bin. "I can't help it," she says. "He drives me insane."

Sawyer closes the recycling bin and joins the girl on the step. He shoves his hands in his pockets and bounces on the balls of his feet. I shrink back into the shadow of the car. I don't think they can see me out here, though in retrospect, I should have chosen Elvira rather than Marilyn.

"If you try to argue with him, he'll engage. He'll bring out his whole *tradition* and *honor* bullshit and use that as an excuse to be a bastard. And everybody else just looks the other way."

She takes a long, angry drag on the cigarette and, as smoke trickles out the corners of her lips, says, "What do you mean, engage?"

Sawyer stops bouncing and turns to face her. I strain to hear. "I mean he'll probably fucking hit you, Kate, okay? So just . . . don't."

I lean forward, as if that'll help me hear them, but a car pulls into the parking lot and their words are muffled by the noise of the tires. It sounds like she says "You marry me, one chicken?"

And while the driver parks, Sawyer says something like "I make you table, butterface."

"Shut up!" I hiss under my breath at the offending car. The driver turns off the engine and gets out.

The girl takes another drag. She and Sawyer just stand there and nod at the guy as he approaches the customer entrance and goes inside.

Kate blows out smoke and drops her cigarette butt to

the ground. She stomps on it and twists it out slowly. "He hit you, then."

"You could say that."

"A lot?"

He shrugs.

"Still?"

"No."

"Because . . . ?"

Sawyer is quiet for a minute. "Because I gave up."

Kate stares at him. "Gave up on what?"

He hesitates, like he's thinking about the answer. "It doesn't matter anymore."

"Come on, tell me."

Sawyer shakes his head. "No. You done? We need to get back in there." He takes the girl gently by the shoulders, turns her around to face the door, opens it, and ushers her in. The door closes hard behind them.

And I stand in the parking lot, dumbfounded. Somebody hit the guy I love. I want to kill whoever it is. But first I have to save my boy. On Valentine's Day.

Fuck.

My phone rings, jolting me back to reality. It's not Trey calling, like I expect. It's Demarco's Pizzeria. Which means it's a parental unit on the other end.

"Crap," I mutter. Customer guy walks back out of

Angotti's with a takeout package as I answer. "Hey," I say, trying to sound breathless. "I left something at the library—my purse. Really important—on the way home now."

There is ominous silence on the other end. I squinch my eyes shut. "Hello?" I say finally.

The normally booming voice is eerily quiet. "Get back here. Now."

"I'm coming!" I start to say, but he hangs up.

I was grounded before. Now it's like I'm the haboob of groundedness. Back at the restaurant, in between tables, Trey gives me concerned looks. My mother is worried that I'm getting addicted to something—it doesn't matter what, she just keeps saying, "Are you addicted?" every twenty minutes. My father goes upstairs as soon as he supergrounds me, apparently overwhelmed by my disobedience, and Rowan looks like she's going to cry because her big sister never used to get into trouble and it's apparently scary as hell for her to see me "like this." Whatever *this* is.

And I'm floored. "All I did was leave for, like, a half hour," I keep explaining. "I came right back. I'm not doing drugs, I'm not *addicted* to anything, I'm not pregnant, people. Jeez." I feel like a broken record. "I'm sixteen, Mom," I say to her. "Do I really have to tell you everything? I think you need to let me grow up a little, and stop . . . hovering."

"Hovering!" she says. "Hovering? As long as you live in this house, I'll hover all I want, thank you very much. We feed you, we give you a warm place to sleep, you have a nice job in the family business, and what do you give back? You go off without telling anybody, you leave your customers, you cavort with that Angotti boy, and you don't appreciate anything we do for you. And then you say 'Stop hovering'?"

I sigh. "Mom, please don't yell. The customers can hear you. I'm sorry. I appreciate you. I should have told somebody I was leaving—I get that. I get that an ordinary worker would be fired for taking off like I did. I just . . . I panicked when I realized I forgot . . . something." I take her hand. "I'm sorry, okay?"

She shakes her head, all worked up. "You are going to be the death of me," she says. "And your father. And your little sister. What kind of example are you?"

Oh, that's so, so nice. "Well, maybe you'd better ask my *little sister*—" I start to say, but then I soften when I see Rowan's face, her wide eyes begging me not to tell her secret.

"Ask her what?" my mother says. "She's not the one in trouble here."

"Ask her . . . why . . ." I falter, unable to think.

Rowan steps up. "Ask me why I didn't tell you she was leaving," she says. "Jules told me she was leaving to look for her . . . thing. And I didn't think to tell you. And she was just . . . being . . . noble by not ratting me out. Or whatever."

I hold Rowan's gaze for a minute, both of us knowing our story sounds ridiculously contrived.

Mom's not buying it. She shakes her head. "You're in cahoots. I don't believe either of you anymore." She turns away and takes her next order from Tony, leaving Rowan and me standing there, afraid to even look at each other. We both disperse and get busy, working like our lives depend on it.

When the rush is over, Trey pulls me aside. "What are you doing?"

I'm tempted to say I'm waiting tables, but the look on his face tells me not to screw around. "Nothing. I don't know. I had to check something so I left. Mom's pissed."

He frowns. "Are you still seeing those . . . crashes?"

"Yes," I say. "And it's just one crash. I see one crash, the same one, over and over. Snowplow hits the back of Angotti's, and the place explodes. Dead bodies. Happy?"

He shoves his hands in his pockets and bites his lip. He can't look at me. "Jules, I think it's time . . ."

"Look, I know what you're thinking. Just give me

through Saturday, okay? If it's still happening on Sunday, I'll do whatever you want. We can tell Mom, I can go see a shrink—whatever you want, okay? Promise. I just need to get through Valentine's Day."

Trey looks into my eyes, and I can tell he's trying to see if I'm lying.

"I mean it," I say. "Please. Just, like, three more days."

"Are you going to follow the house rules and stop doing weird shit?"

I hesitate. "I can't say for sure," I say quietly. "And I also don't think I'm crazy, Trey. Not anymore."

His forehead wrinkles in alarm. "Oh, that's just great."

"No, I know what you're thinking, but I feel perfectly normal otherwise. I think . . . okay, this is going to sound really weird, I know, but I think I'm seeing something that hasn't happened yet. Something that's going to happen. Like a psychic thing." I pause, trying to gauge his reaction. "So when this event does happen . . . it should hopefully all be over for good." *Unless there's another crash after this.* . . . But I don't say that. I can't stand the thought of that. Besides, I need to get through this one first.

Trey looks dubious. Finally he says, "How do you know it's happening on Valentine's?"

I bite my lip and look down at the carpet. Shake my

head. "I'm still figuring it out. But I promise I'll tell you once I do know. Deal?" *Please.*

He sighs heavily and throws his hands in the air. "Sure, whatever. Okay. So Sunday, we're telling Mom."

I grip his forearms and grin wide. "Yes. Thank you."

"Just . . . be safe, okay? I'm watching you. Don't go anywhere without telling me. Or, I know—why don't you just stay home like you're supposed to."

I nod to appease him, and for the first time in my life, I look my dear brother, my best friend, in the eye, and I lie my face off. "I will."

Twenty-Eight

When I finally get a free minute, I step outside to take out the trash and call Angotti's using star 67 to hide my number, knowing it's a lost cause but feeling like I have to try. Luckily, a woman answers.

"Angotti's!"

"Good evening. I need a reservation for eight people this Saturday night at seven," I say, trying to sound rich and important.

She nearly laughs. "For Valentine's Day? We've been booked solid for weeks. The only time I have open is at eleven in the morning. I'm very sorry."

I squinch my eyes shut. "I can assure you we'll make it worth your while. I need the two window tables, please. Seven p.m. Six forty-five would also work if seven isn't available."

She hesitates. "I'm very sorry, ma'am, but it's really not possible. We're booked."

"I'm a big customer," I say. "May I please speak to the owner? Perhaps we can work something out so I don't have to take my business elsewhere."

She clears her throat impatiently, and I know now it's Sawyer's mother and I'm toast. "I *am* one of the owners," she says, and I hear the authority rising in her voice, yet she remains calm. "And I'm sorry, but as I said, and as I continue to say, we are booked solid. I am unable to fulfill your needs at that particular time. Perhaps you'd like to come in Friday or Sunday evening instead?"

Trey peeks his head out the door and I wave him off. "I'm afraid that won't work. Thanks anyway." I hang up before she can respond, and then I go back inside. My mind won't stop.

At one thirty in the morning I'm still lying awake, thinking, trying to figure out all the pieces of the puzzle. And all I know is that I just have to try one more time to convince Sawyer to believe me. And there's only one way I can think of to do that right now.

By two I've managed to sneak out without waking anybody up, and I'm standing behind Angotti's Trattoria, hoping the beat cop doesn't decide to come by right now. I whip my head around when an icicle crashes off the building, and my stomach buzzes. It's warming up to the low thirties or so, according to the forecast, and the weekend snow is about to start. Out here, before the snow falls, it's so quiet that you'd never know we're in a suburb of the third-largest city in the United States.

I'm standing three feet from the window that will shatter. Four from the tables where the people will be sitting. I can see the clock inside thanks to the emergency lighting, and I synchronize my old Mickey Mouse watch.

Out here, a few feet to the left of the window, there's an old gas meter and line that goes into the building— something I hadn't been able to get close enough to see before now—and I guess that the kitchen is on the other side of it. It's where the truck hits. That explains the explosion. I wonder what ignites everything once the gas flows freely. Or does it happen inside, maybe? I don't really know. I don't understand gas lines.

I stare at the back of the building, mesmerized, picturing everything and how it will happen.

In my hand is my cell phone. I've been holding it for practically an hour, debating, not daring to intrude again and risk rejection once more. But finally I do it. I have to. I call him, hoping he keeps his phone on all night like I keep mine. Hoping I don't wake the whole family. Hoping.

It rings five times in my ear, and then it clicks. He says in a deep, sleepy voice, "Yeah?"

"Hi," I say softly, and I realize I didn't plan this out. "It's . . . it's me. Can you, um, come down? Out back?" I'm an idiot.

I hear a whoosh of breath, and feedback like his phone jostles, like he's sitting up in bed, like he's confused and thinking, and I expect a multitude of exasperated questions like "Who is this?" and "Are you insane?" But those don't come.

A light in a window above me turns on, and I suck in a breath and crouch down against the block wall as if being smaller will hide me from the light.

A moment later he's back. "Yeah," he says. "Be there in a minute."

And it's like we're in sixth grade again, and no time has passed, and we're standing by our lockers planning what time we're going to meet under the slide on the elementary school playground.

The phone goes dead. I keep it to my ear for a few seconds, and then lower it and put it in my pocket. Tiny bits of snow begin to float down, or maybe they were there for a while and I just noticed them. I shiver and do a mental count. Forty-one hours to go.

A few minutes later, carefully and almost silently, a figure emerges from the building, and Sawyer Angotti, the guy I've loved since first grade, comes over to me.

I stand up. Look up at him, at his sleepy eyes. He holds

a finger to his lips, tugs my coat sleeve, and gestures to the far street, whose name I don't know. We walk together without speaking. When we get to the sidewalk along the road, he just puts his hands on my shoulders and looks into my eyes. "Oh, Jules," he says, shaking his head. "What are you doing?" He gives me the half grin that almost kills me.

I swallow hard. Glad he's not mad. "I had to come one last time to talk to you."

He nods, resigned to listen. "All right, then. Go."

I look down at the sidewalk. "Something bad is going to happen here," I say, as painfully aware of his hands on my shoulders as I am of the fact that he's not believing me, and for the millionth time I doubt myself and my own sanity. "I know when it's going to happen now. Valentine's night, 7:04 p.m." I continue talking, staring blindly at his slipper shoes. "I know you don't believe me, and it's okay with me if the whole school thinks I'm insane. I just need to ask you to please be careful, and if there's any way you can *not* be in the building or in this back parking lot at 7:04 p.m. on Saturday night, just even, you know, step outside the front door for a few minutes . . . please . . ." I bite my lip to stop my voice from pitching higher, into frantic mode. I can't look him in the eye.

I hear him sigh, feel its weight in his hands on my shoulders. He rests his chin on my bowed head for a moment and pulls me closer, into him. And then he moves his face next to mine. He smells like a man now. I wonder how long it's been since he smelled like a boy.

My eyes close, but all I can do is stand there numbly. I wasn't expecting this response, and I don't know what to do with my hands—they hang stiffly at my sides. I want to wrap my arms around him, hold him, but I don't. I can't.

As we stand there together, bodies nearer than they've ever been before, I wonder how many times I will regret not holding him.

Twenty-Nine

The saddest part, the part that makes the tears rush out of the corners of my eyes as I lie in bed an hour later, staring at the ceiling, is that he thinks listening to me is enough, and believing me is too much.

In school Friday I can't help but look for him, and I find him looking for me, his melancholy eyes sending me a weird, pitying glance, like he's trying to empathize, and it only frustrates me.

I get it now. He's being Sawyer, the guy who is nice to the outcasts—one of my favorite things about him. That's the kid, the guy, I've always loved. But I never, ever wanted to be the target. I wanted to be the partner. He believes he's protecting me in a way, but it feels like he's leading me on with his listening ear, trying to be there for an old friend who's losing her marbles. He even sends me a text message. "You doing okay? We should talk at lunch. Under the slide? ☺"

And that about does me in. I can't even answer it, because when he's dead, I want this to be the only text in the thread on my phone.

Dear dog, I'm such a mess.

He finds me at the drinking fountain.

"Hey!" he says in a strangely cheerful voice. His smile isn't the one from last night. It's the volunteer smile, the good-student smile. The fake smile.

"Hi," I say with as much enthusiasm as I can. I bite my lip, wondering when, between two in the morning and now, things actually changed for him. When he became distant, nice-guy Sawyer, and if he regrets going down to meet me in the middle of the night when he might not have been thinking straight.

"You doing okay?"

I smile and nod. "Mm-hmm. You?"

"A little tired." He laughs.

My heart is breaking. I don't want to be in this conversation. I don't want to be his animal shelter favorite. I'd rather be ignored than that. "Yeah," I say. My laugh is hollow, and I wonder if he notices.

"Hey, about last night," he says, lowering his voice

considerably. "I probably can't ever do that again, okay? So maybe don't . . . come over. Anymore. It's just a bad idea, you know? The family thing and all." His face is strained, about to crack from the perma-smile. "I'd get in a lot of trouble if I got caught."

"Sure, yeah," I say. "Yeah, no, I won't do that ever again. It was definitely a one time thing." I turn my head, looking for a distraction so I can get out of here. "Just did it for old times' sake, I guess. I don't know. It was dumb."

He relaxes a little, and the awkwardness, still there, has a veil over it now. "Okay, cool." He shuffles his feet, suddenly at a loss for words. He points with his thumb down the hallway. "I'm supposed to be meeting . . . someone . . ."

"Of course, yeah. Go. Good to see you." I wave him away and turn back to the drinking fountain.

"And—" he says in a smiley, awkward voice. "And, um, I'm not actually going to be working Valentine's Day anyway. I'll be at the dance. So, you know, whatever that thing is you're worried about, well, you don't need to worry anymore, 'cause it's cool."

I stare at the stream of water in front of me, not thinking about anything except the fact that this is my last good-bye with him, and it sucks. I don't look at him. "Okay, great."

He hesitates and then starts walking away, and I'm cursing myself because this isn't how I want it to end. Not like this at all. These words of sheer idiocy cannot be our last words.

I let go of the spigot and stand up. "Hey, Sawyer?"

He stops and turns back, and the fake shit is gone from his face. "Yeah?"

I press my lips together and thread my fingers, bringing my hands up to my chest nervously, and then I smile while everything breaks inside. "It's okay," I say, nodding, and I can feel my bottom lip quivering anyway. "It's okay that you don't believe me. I'll leave you alone now. I really do love you, like I said the other . . . that one time. The other day. I just want you to know that."

He stands there, his face stricken and real, and falling. He opens his mouth as if to speak, and then closes it again, and pain I've never seen before washes across it. He nods once, says, "Okay, thanks," and then he turns away and walks slowly toward the cafeteria, ripping his fingers through his hair as he goes.

Thirty

When he's out of sight, I go the other way on numb, stupid feet, all the way to my locker, and I stand there not knowing what to do with myself now. I open a book and there are no words, only scenes screaming at me. There's nothing I can do today anymore. I have to get out of here. I have to go away. I can't see him again.

There are two periods left in my day, and I will spend them in the meatball truck, waiting for Rowan to come. That's the only thing I can think of doing right now.

I grab my books like I always do on Fridays, as if I'm going to get any studying done this weekend, and head out to the truck. There's a teacher on rat patrol at the entrance, and I walk right by him. "Orthodontist appointment," I say, even though I got my braces off two years ago. Worked like a charm then, and it does now, too. He doesn't even try to stop me.

When I push through the door, it's snowing.

I walk to the truck, the cold flakes kissing my cheeks and making my eyelashes heavy. This is the beginning of the snow that I see in the vision, I think. The beginning of the end. Thirty hours to go. I get into the truck and start it up, letting it run for a few minutes to get some heat going, sit back to wait for the weather report on the radio, and close my eyes to figure out how the hell I'm going to shut that restaurant down and save nine people's lives.

And then my eyes spring open, and it finally hits me, what Sawyer said. He said he's not going to be there. He's going to the dance.

He's going to the fucking dance, and he's not going to be at Angotti's.

So how the heck is he ending up in a body bag? Does he come home for some reason that he doesn't expect? Does he get a frantic call and return to the restaurant, and something happens after? Does he go in to save someone and die that way?

"Oh. My. Fucking. Dogs!" I yell, and pound the steering wheel. "What the hell is going on? Why can't you just tell me what's happening? Tell me what to do, whoever, whatever, you are! Ugh!" I slam my body back into the seat and scream at the top of my lungs, way back here in the last row of the parking lot, where no one can hear me.

Maybe I am insane.

Maybe I really am.

Maybe this vision means nothing at all, except that I am losing it.

Around and around we go again. Again. Again.

I don't have time for this.

As the snow builds up on my windshield faster than it can melt, things grow cold and dusky inside my truck, and the vision plays out more clearly on the glass. Teeth chattering, I start up the truck again, flip the wipers on, and whisk the snow away, realizing it's coming down majorly hard right now. So hard that I wonder aloud, "If this doesn't stop, is it going to be too much?" A few minutes later the weather report is in—a blizzard watch, and it calls for twelve to eighteen inches in the greater Chicago area over the next twelve hours.

"Jeez," I mutter. I've seen my share of snowstorms, and one foot of snow is actually way more than a foot of snow when it has to be removed from half the city and put into the other half. If this pace keeps up, the fire hydrant will be covered in the first plowing.

The facts race through my head. Too much snow. Sawyer not working. Nothing's adding up right to fit the vision. *Maybe I do need to be committed to a hospital,* I think for the millionth time. I give up on it as Rowan trudges through the snow and gets into the truck.

"You're here early," she says.

I put the truck in drive and hit the gas, trying to beat the rush of students. "Yep."

Rowan just looks at me, and then she says earnestly, "What's wrong with you, Jules? What have you really been doing?"

I glance over at her, and she looks scared for me.

"Nothing. I'm fine." I turn the corner and then peek at her again. "Really." She doesn't say anything, so I reach over and pinch her kneecap, which she hates. And then I grin at her. "Seriously, kid. I'm fine. Things are really kind of bizarro world right now. Mom and Dad are cracking down on me for dumb stuff, but I messed up, too, by leaving customers without telling anybody, and that was dumb of me. And nice of you to try to cover, even though it didn't work. But other than that, we're all fine. 'Kay?"

"Okay," she says dubiously, and leans her head against the side window. "I just hate it when everybody's too quiet or too loud."

"Yeah, me too." I turn the wipers on high as we truck along, and turn the radio up so we can hear it against the beat and squeak of the wipers and the roar of the defroster.

I peer out through the windshield, trying to ignore the vision. "Dang, it's nasty out here."

"Maybe we'll get a snow day tomorrow," Rowan says, excitement in her voice. "Oh, wait."

"Yeah," I say. "Saturday. That's the breaks."

"Work is going to suck."

"It always does on Valentine's Day," I say. And I have to angle my head away from her because tears pop to my eyes. "It's really going to suck this year."

"Because of Sawyer? You like him, don't you? That's what everybody's mad about. Right?"

I think about that as I turn into the alley and park the truck, and we sit and wait for Trey to get here so we can enter as a force as usual. "I guess you could say that. But he doesn't like me, so it's not a problem."

"I think he does."

"What do you know?"

"He follows you around, he watches you. I see him."

I turn to look at her. "He does not."

She shrugs. "Hey, I'm not blind. But like you said, it's better if he doesn't like you."

I frown. Rowan is sneakier than she looks. But this news just makes everything worse. The aching crevasse in my chest opens up a little more. "Hurry up, Trey," I mutter.

Finally he comes and we all go inside. It's 4:04. I

have exactly twenty-seven hours to figure out what I'm supposed to do.

"I wonder what kind of crowd we'll get tonight," Mom says cheerily. "Look at it coming down."

Mom and the three of us kids stand at the front entrance as it nears five o'clock, ready and waiting for the early birds, but not sure if they'll come out tonight or if they're all at the grocery store stocking up on toilet paper. I feel like we could make a public service announcement letting Chicagoland know that if they need anything, anything at all, we probably have it upstairs.

"We're going to be slammed with deliveries, I bet," Rowan says. She's the queen of gauging delivery orders.

We all agree, mesmerized by the heavy flakes. I shake my head and turn away, going into the dining room to make sure everything's ready for the brave souls who venture out, and it is, of course. I plop down in a booth and stare out the window, wondering what Sawyer's doing right now. If he's remembering our awkward conversation, or trying to forget it. Wondering what'll happen, and how. My stomach churns as now, in all of our windows, the vision plays out over and over, and I can't get away from it. It plays out on the front of the menus, too, and the paper place mats on the tables, and the computer screen up at the cash wrap. The urgency of the vision is coming through loud and clear. "Okay, okay," I mutter. "I know already."

I twist the heels of my hands into my eyes, trying to rid them of the vision, feeling myself slipping back into that place of hopelessness. Nothing's right. Nothing is what I expected. Nothing is as it seems. I think that if I were a comic book character, I'd have the most desolate story of a wasted life—a wannabe hero who doesn't come through for the victims. The end.

When I feel a hand on my shoulder, I look up. My mom squeezes my arm and then slides into the booth across from me. She's always been pretty, but she looks older than she is. She has dark circles under her eyes, like me.

She puts her elbows on the table and rests her chin in her hands, gazing at me. "Where'd you go last night?" she asks.

I hesitate, suspicious. "To the library. I told Dad—"

"No, I mean in the middle of the night."

I lean back in the booth, trying to keep a poker face, but I wasn't expecting this. "Oh."

She nods, waiting.

And really, what does it matter now? On Monday we're going to have another talk. And I'm going to end up in the hospital with scary people. So I tell her the truth. Sort of. "I went to see Sawyer Angotti, to say good-bye."

She is silent. And then she takes my hands and holds them and says, "I'm very sorry about that, Julia."

I tilt my head, perplexed, and really look at her. She *is* sorry. I can see it. Wow. "Thanks," I say. "That was . . . unexpected."

She smiles grimly, collapsing her arms onto the table, and sits back in the booth. "You're not the first person who's had to say good-bye to an Angotti. I imagine it's hard. Some of them are actually decent people, even if they make mistakes."

I stare. "What . . . you?"

The bell over the door tinkles with the first dinner customer, and she gets up to take the hostess stand tonight. "No, not me."

"You mean Dad?"

But she doesn't answer me. Instead, she says, "Why don't you take tonight off? You could use a break."

Thirty-One

Upstairs, I can't do anything. The windows are plastered with the scenes. So are the mirrors. The scenes dance around the pile of Christmas tins, play out on every board game cover, every magazine, every newspaper. Every schoolbook I open screams explosions at me. There are no words, only the crash. The crash is my life.

Sitting in the chair as it gets dark, I think about checking myself into the hospital. I don't even know if I can drive when all the windows are playing the scenes. I can't concentrate on anything, it's getting so bad. I can't imagine it being any worse. And finally, I wonder if maybe it's trying to tell me something *else*.

Maybe it's trying to scream at me that I've got the facts right . . . and the date wrong.

And that I'm an idiot.

And that this. *Crash*. Event. *Crash*. Is imminent. *EXPLOSION.*

I lean forward in the chair with a gasp, pressing my fingers into my temples and squeezing my eyes shut. All this crap circulating in my brain is making everything harder to comprehend, and it's a stupid shame that I haven't figured it out before now. But with this snow, it's got to be. "Maybe," I muse. "Maybe they put the decorations up *this morning*. And maybe Sawyer is working *tonight*. No doubt he is, he's got tomorrow off . . . and the snow . . ." I slam my body back into the living room chair with a groan, knocking a box of recipes off the table next to me, and then scramble to my feet to check the time. "Holy shit."

Because with these facts—the snow forecast, Sawyer not working—this crash cannot happen tomorrow night. It's happening tonight.

It's 5:42 when I realize that I do not have twenty-five hours and twenty-two minutes to save the world. I have one hour and twenty-two minutes.

ONE HOUR. TWENTY-TWO MINUTES.

My hands start to shake and my throat goes dry. The scenes from the vision are no longer attached to windows and walls and screens and books, but they swirl around me, giving me vertigo. I grab the wall to steady myself, and then I go to the phone, because the only thing that screams in my ears right now is the conversation I had with Sawyer's mother yesterday when I was trying to get a reservation. *How about Friday or Sunday? Friday or Sunday? Friday or Sunday?*

I have the wherewithal to dial star 67, and then yank the restaurant's phone number from somewhere in my memory, because I certainly can't look it up right now. When a young woman answers, I say in the same voice as the one I used yesterday, "Hello, there. Any chance I can make a reservation for tonight? Party of eight, seven p.m.?"

"Sure, one moment. I think we had a cancellation."

I keep my eyes closed to stop the spinning, and count every second that goes by.

She comes back. "All right, no problem. Last name?"

My eyes spring open and I have to hold myself back from blurting out my real name. "Uh . . . Kravitz."

"Kravitz? Seven o'clock. You're all set."

I almost shout, "Can we have the window tables?"

She hesitates. "Um, sure," she says, and I think I may have scared her.

I force myself to speak calmly. "Thank you. Thank you so very much. You'll have the tables ready right on time, right? We won't be able to wait." My head is aching.

"Of course, Ms. Kravitz. We'll take good care of you."

"Thank you."

We hang up, and I feel like the band around my chest

has loosened slightly. When I open my eyes, things have slowed down. In fact, something's quite different. I lunge for the TV remote and turn it on, hitting slow motion immediately. And there it is. The difference. I pause it, hands shaking.

On the window scene, the tables are empty, and on the last scene, something else is different. Now in the body bag scene there are only four bags.

Only four! One phone call saved five people's lives. "Holy mother of crap," I whisper as I stare at the new frame.

But Sawyer's dead face remains.

Thirty-Two

Despite staring at Sawyer's dead face, I feel a surge of hope. The swirling scenes around me have calmed down, as if I'm being rewarded for figuring something out, for getting something right. I glance at my watch and try not to freak out. My next move is figuring out how to get my grounded ass out of here without being noticed. But first . . .

"I need you," I text to Trey, and then I turn on the computer. Everything I see is the new crash vision.

In less than two minutes, I hear the pounding—Trey taking the steps two at a time. He bursts into the apartment. "You okay?"

"So far. Can you do something for me?"

"What is it?"

"Search 'exterior gas valve shutoff.' Hurry."

He only hesitates a split second, and then he does it, but the computer takes agonizingly long to load anything. "Why am I doing this?"

"Because I can't see the web pages. I only see the crash."

"Oh, God, that's so weird."

"Please hurry."

"I'm trying," he mutters, shaking the mouse side to side. "You'd think Dad could start collecting newer models of computers, but no, that's too logical." The minutes tick away, and he types and taps his fingers on the desk. "Here it comes, finally," he says, and then reads everything he finds about shutoff valves.

I jiggle, nervous energy pulsing through me. He can't read fast enough. "Okay, thank you. Trey?"

"Yes?"

"I love you."

He looks at me. "Jesus, Jules. What are you doing?"

I bite my lip. "I have to go out for a bit. The crash—I think it's happening tonight." I want to say more, but I can't. I need him to say something. Something big, so I know he's on my side.

He doesn't move. Only his eyes flit back and forth on mine. "Tell me everything," he says finally.

I glance at the clock and jump to my feet. It's after six. "I don't have time. It's happening at 7:04 p.m." I glide through the piles of junk to my room and grab the Elvira wig. "I gotta go." I slip my arms around his waist and hug him.

He hugs back. "But, Jules, this is cra—I mean, this is, ah . . ."

"It's okay if you don't believe me," I find myself saying for the second time today. "I just have to do this, and I'll—I'll see you later. I'll be at Angotti's. Don't tell them—Mom and Dad—unless . . . unless it's absolutely necessary."

"Jules, you're talking scary. Just sit tight, okay? Stay here. I'm going to get Mom."

"Trey," I say, and I've never been more calm. "If you stop me from saving Sawyer Angotti, I will never, ever forgive you. If I'm actually crazy right now, nothing will happen to Angotti's or to me, and I'll be fine, and you can tell Mom everything then. But if I'm not crazy, and this crash is really about to happen, I have to do something. I have to. I can't *not* do it. I have a feeling this vision thing won't totally leave me until it's all over, but it calms down when I do the right thing. And right now, I'm doing the right thing—that's all I'm sure of." I look at him. "I need you to keep Mom and Dad from noticing that I'm gone, or I'm totally screwed. Okay?"

He shakes his head at me, a perplexed look on his face. "Jesus, Jules." He leans over and grips the back of the desk chair and gives it a little shake.

"You said that already." I grab his arm. "Trey, come on. Don't doubt me. You know me. I'm not insane." *Is it a lie? I guess we'll find out.*

"We should call the police, then," he says, turning back to face me.

"And tell them what? That a crash is about to happen? Yeah, that'll work." Worry grips his face, and I totally understand why, but I'm running out of time. All the muscles in my body are twitching, urging me to go out the door, but my brain tells me I have to get at least one person to sort of believe me or everything else will be messed up.

He just shakes his head, and I can hear his phone vibrating in his pocket. He checks it. "Mom," he says. He gives me an urgent look. "Okay," he says finally. "I'll cover for you. Just don't do anything stupid, don't be Superman, and call me immediately when it's . . . over. Or whatever. Right?"

Electricity surges through me, like I've won a battle. "Thanks. I'll call you. I promise!" I grab my wig, coat, and keys and fly to the door.

"Wait," he says. He looks around the dining room frantically. "Hold up a sec. You need . . ." He spies something and goes to it, wrestling a red box from the middle of a pile of junk. He pulls it out, causing an avalanche, and opens it—it's a toolbox. "You need this," he says, handing me a wrench. "For the gas valve. A quarter turn will shut it off. Do it and get the hell out of there. Promise me."

I take the wrench. "Promise." I reach up and grab him around the neck, giving him a quick kiss on the cheek, which he doesn't even wipe off. "See you in a bit." And then I turn and go down the steps as quietly as I can and escape out the door to the alley and hop into my giant meatball truck.

On my wristwatch: Both white-gloved Mickey Mouse hands point at the six. Thirty-four minutes to explosion. Way too much time wasted. I wind the giant meatballs around town, and the route that normally takes me just under five minutes takes twice as long because of the snow and the cars. I want to barrel right over them. "Hurry up!" I scream, shaking the steering wheel. Finally I drive past Angotti's, and my suspicion is confirmed. The decorations are up now—giant puffy crepe-paper pendant-like hearts that look like . . . well, apparently they look like light fixtures from far away. The Angottis must have hung them this morning.

But I don't have time to ponder trivial things. I drive to the street where the snowplow will come from. At 6:41, I park a couple blocks away so nobody sees my truck.

I take out my cell phone and text Sawyer, not caring what he'll think of me when he gets the message. "I was wrong. The explosion is TONIGHT at 7:04. Please,

Sawyer . . . I won't bother you again, I just had to tell you. Get out of there."

I don't have time to wait for a reply. I grab the wrench, shove the wig on my head, and fly out of the truck and down the street in the snow. I pass the sign and glance at the fire hydrant across the street. The snow level isn't right—it's too low—and I almost stop, but the vision's frequency ramps up when I start to slow down, so I keep going. I reach the back of the building and sneak along it, edging under the window, praying that nobody comes out the back door right now.

When I get to the gas meter, it's covered in snow. I wipe it clean and look for the lever that Trey described to me. Finally I find it, but it's encased in ice. I try to break the ice around it with my hands, but it doesn't budge. I chip away at the ice with the Crescent wrench, cringing at every noise it makes. Sweat pours from under my wig as I whip my gloves off to get a better grasp on the joints around the lever, and I can't even think about how much time is passing because it just makes my fingers fumble. At one point the wrench slips and splits open my knuckle. "Faaaaahck," I mutter. But I keep going, blood and all.

Finally the lever is free. I glance at my watch and frantically figure out the timing. If I turn the gas off too soon, their stoves will go out and they'll come out and check on it at just the wrong time. *So many ways for people to die here,* I think.

My watch says 6:53. I close my eyes, my thighs quaking from sitting on my haunches for so long, my finger still bleeding and starting to throb. Gingerly I put my gloves back on, watching a stain form in the cloth, but there's no time to worry about something so trivial now. I still haven't figured out how to save Sawyer and the other three.

I glance at a window of a nearby house and watch the scene. If Sawyer believes me and plans to get out of there, my bet is that his body bag will disappear. But it only takes a few seconds to find out that there are still four dead from this event. "Come on, Sawyer," I whisper. "Believe me."

It's 6:56, and I'm still sitting here. My phone buzzes in my pocket but I can't look at it. When I hear a rumbling, I look up and almost wet my pants. A snowplow is barreling up the road in my direction, eight minutes early. I shake my watch in case it stopped, but the second hand keeps ticking away.

A second later I realize the truck is going slower than the one in the vision, and its plow is engaged. It hits me now—in the vision, the road is freshly plowed, and the out-of-control truck has its plow up. This is not the same truck. I breathe a sigh of relief and mop my sweaty forehead.

The plow reaches the end of the road, sweeps around, and does the other side. The snow pummels the sides of the road, reaching the top of the fire hydrant and a third of the way up the signpost. If I weren't so freaked out, I'd be amazed at the way everything is coming together.

As soon as 6:59 hits, I take the wrench, engage it with the lever, and pull until it's crosswise from the pipe, a quarter turn. And then I get to my feet and run like hell, hoping it'll take at least five minutes for the kitchen to figure out the ovens aren't firing.

It takes me less than a minute to run the two blocks back to the truck, and I'm using some strange superpower energy that I don't normally have. Chest heaving, I climb in, start it up, and hit the gas. I barrel over the pile of snow left by the recent plowing and drive to Angotti's and into their parking lot. It feels eerily like what the snowplow will be doing in about three minutes.

Then I stop the truck and just look at this crazy scene, so familiar, so freaking spooky. All the cars are in exactly the right places, the lighting and snow are right, the tables I reserved are empty. I stare for a second, amazed at how everything is exactly as it is in the vision. It's like being in some weird *Twilight Zone* episode. But I have no more than a second to ponder it, because I'm still not sure exactly what I'm going to do with this truck.

What I'd like to do is park it in the path of the snowplow and make a run for it, but then it'll plow my truck into the restaurant too, so I know I'll have to gun it as it hits me to try to spin the plow. I pull up into that area just to see what happens, and now there are five body bags in the vision. That's obviously not the way to go. I back up and the bags number four again. "Jeez," I mutter, checking my watch: 7:02. "A little help here, please."

I grip the steering wheel and get no inkling, no clue from the vision god. "Ugh!" I yell. "Don't do this to me!" But the vision just plays in my side mirror, not giving me any help at all. I peer down the road and suck in a few breaths, trying to keep my hands from shaking, and back up a little farther.

Before I can check the vision again to see if my move changed anything, I see a dark figure running toward me. For a second I'm paralyzed, unsure of whom this could be, because there is no scene like this in the vision. Then my passenger door opens and Trey hops into the truck. "Nice hair," he says, breathing hard. He slams the door shut.

"What are you doing?" I scream at him. "You have to get out!"

"I can't let you do this," he says. "Do you know what you're doing?"

The vision plays brightly on the windshield like a warning, and suddenly there are five body bags again. "Shit," I say. "Shit! Trey, get *out*. You're going to die if you don't get out of here!"

He stares at me and puts his seat belt on. My watch says 7:03.

"Fuck, Trey, I'm serious. Get out! The snowplow will be coming from there in one minute," I scream, pointing, "and you'll get crushed!" I can't scream any louder.

"Just calm it down, Demarco!" he yells back, and then he softens. "I can't let you do this alone. What if you're one of the people who ends up dead? How would I live with that, huh, Jules? Did you think of that? Just don't get T-boned."

I stare at him hard. "Don't get T-boned," I whisper. And then I see it in my head—I'm doing it wrong. I need to sideswipe the plow, not let it hit me full-on. I whip the truck into reverse. "You're brilliant, you stupid jerk."

"I know," he says.

I barrel around to the back of the lot and turn my truck to face the restaurant, parallel to the road. I'll be able to get a moving start alongside the plow, then angle into it where it jumps the curb to steer it back to the street, where it belongs. "Okay," I say. "Get into the middle seat and strap in, you stubborn fuck. I got this. Shit, damn, hell! It's 7:04."

There's no time to focus on the mirror, and I can't afford to lose my concentration now. No time to know if this is a winning plan or not, I just have to do it. I suck in a deep breath and grip the wheel tighter, watching for it, rolling forward slightly to get traction.

"Oh my God, look . . . ," Trey says, the words trailing off. His head is turned and he's looking behind us out the window. He points and his voice turns to wonder. "Holy crap, Jules. You were right. Here it comes." He turns and gives me a look of utter terror. "You're going to have to gun it!"

Thirty-Three

I glance at the restaurant one last time and see Kate, the smoking girl, coming outside. "No," I shout, though there's no way she can hear me. "Get back!" She must be one of the people in the body bags, I realize with a pang. I ease onto the gas so we gain speed without spinning out, just before the snowplow jounces over the curb and the snow. By the time it comes up alongside me, we are moving well, and I edge my nose in front of it, hanging on for the initial jolt. The snowplow's not slowing, and I have to floor it to stay in front. I tap it twice more. "It's not moving over!" I scream, and then I swerve hard into it, breaking Trey's window. It's bumper cars for the big leagues.

"Shit!" Everything goes in slow motion. My insides

quake and slam against each other. My head bangs
against my window and then cracks into Trey's head,
but I feel no pain. The hood of our meatball truck flies
open as I find the gas pedal again and gun it once more,
blinded but trying with all my might to push the plow
away from the building. "Help me!" I scream. "I can't
hold it! I can't see!"

Trey grabs the wheel and together we crank it, and I
catch a glimpse of the snowplow driver's head smashing
against his window and flopping forward, his body held up
only by his seat belt.

"Hang on!" Trey yells.

The grinding sound of metal on metal makes my head
want to explode. I lean left to try to look around the hood,
seeing the restaurant window and the blond girl safely off
to my left. "We're doing it!" I yell.

A split second later all I can see from my side window
is a brick wall coming at me. I try to get away from it,
leaning my head toward Trey, but momentum is against
me and the rest of me won't follow. I feel my body pressing
hard against my door, against my will.

When the plow slams us into the corner of the restaurant, there is an enormous crunching sound, and pressure, pressure. Pressure.

All goes black.

•   •   •

Sirens. All I hear are emergency sirens trying to play a song, but nobody gets the tune right. I want them to play a song I know, but they don't listen to me. They can't hear me.

In the background of the horrible siren song is the vision, playing slow, and I can see through everything like they are ghosts. It's a different story now. The snowplow speeds toward the restaurant, swerving to the wrong side of the road, jumping the curb, where a food truck in the back of a mostly empty parking lot speeds to meet it. The truck noses in front of the plow, trying to guide it away from the restaurant, but the plow doesn't help it. The food truck turns sharply, smashes its passenger side into the side of the snowplow. A smoking girl watches dumbfounded from the back step of the restaurant, about to be smashed to bits, yet frozen, unable to move. A young man in the window stares wide-eyed. He checks his watch, drops settings on an empty table, and runs.

The food truck makes a last grand effort to push the plow away from the building, and finally it succeeds, just barely. But there's not enough room for both vehicles to clear it. The food truck slams into the corner of the building as the snowplow is forced to turn toward the road. It ramps up the hood of a parked car, tips over it, and lands with a shudder on its side, sliding and coming to rest in a quiet intersection. The food truck, wrapped around the corner of the building, is bent like an elbow and hissing. Two giant meatballs have snapped off and soar through the air, coming to an abrupt rest in a snowbank.

No one moves.

The smoking girl comes to life. She makes a phone call with shaky hands and opens the door from which she came, screaming for help.

When red and blue lights make the evening glow, two body bags lie in the snow.

A moment later, one of them disappears.

The vision ends before the wheels of the snowplow stop spinning.

Thirty-Four

I hear things. People talking, shouting. I hear a familiar voice, but I can't place it. For a second I open my eyes, looking for the vision in the shattered, blood-spattered windshield and not seeing it. A voice shouts my name. But it's very noisy there. I have to close my eyes and go back to where it's quiet again.

Every time I open my eyes, I hear the shouting and the screeching and the buzzing, and I can't stand it. I need to get away from it. My stomach hurts and I feel like I am in a lot of trouble. I snuck out again. My father is going to be so mad. But I can't think for long because I have to get away.

• • •

When I wake up, an animal is attacking my face. I try to reach for it but only one of my arms moves. I grab the animal and pull its skinny legs out of my nose, but that only hurts more. I have to get out of there. I have to get it off me. I hear noises again, but it's all muffled—everything is muffled, and I wonder if my wig has slipped down over my ears.

Somebody holds my arm and I go back to sleep.

The next time I wake up, I just open my eyes and stare at the weird ceiling above me. For a moment I wonder if Dad did something to our bedroom. I frown at it, puzzled. I try to swallow and my throat hurts. I blink a few times, not quite sure if I'm going to get out of bed today, but I know I probably have a test or something . . . or wait, no—it's a food holiday so it'll be busy. I have to work. I brace my right hand on the bed to try and scoot myself up to sitting, but I'm just too tired. I'll try again later.

"Julia?"

I turn my head slowly and see my mother. She looks terrible. "What's happening?" My voice comes out all raspy.

She nods and smiles, tears in her eyes, dark circles even darker below them. "You were in an accident. You're in the hospital. How do you feel?" There's a noise from another part of the room and I turn my head in slow motion. Nothing wants to move today. It's my father, and

I'm too tired to be scared. Rowan is back there too, I see.

"I'm okay," I say. And before I can say "What happened?" bits of things rush back to my memory. I struggle to sit up, alarmed, but it hurts so much to move. "Where's Trey?"

"He's at home," Mom hurries to explain, reaching out and gently pushing my shoulders back down. "He's fine. He just got banged up, some cuts and bruises. He's sleeping. He's . . . he's fine."

I fall back in relief, and then vaguely I remember the last vision. "So . . . who's dead? Is it Sawyer?" I close my eyes, and in spite of the fuzziness in my brain, pain sears through my chest. "Oh, God. Not Sawyer." I don't care if my father's listening.

"Honey," my mother says, "you just need to rest now, okay? Don't get all worked up."

"You have to tell me. I know someone's dead. Who is it?"

Rowan comes over to the other side of the bed and touches my shoulder. "It's not Sawyer," she says. "He's fine." She gives me a look like she wants to say more but can't.

I sigh as much as my body lets me, which isn't very much, and I'm exhausted again. "Thank you," I whisper. Good old Rowan.

Mom holds a glass of water for me and I drink some from a straw. Everything takes so long to do.

My father just stands there, looking like a big oaf.

I gaze at him under half-closed lids. "I'm sorry about the truck," I say, and tears start spilling, not just from my eyes, but his, too. I haven't seen him cry in a long time.

He comes closer and takes my hand. "The truck doesn't matter," he says. "You matter. I'm glad you're going to be okay." He swallows hard and then says in a gruff voice, "You saved a lot of people. I don't know if you know what you did."

I almost laugh. "I have an idea," I whisper. I want to know more, but my eyes won't stay open, and once again everything is dark and quiet.

When I wake up again, I am alone. I open my eyes cautiously, expecting to see scene after scene reflected in the monitors and windows, but there are none. Instead, there are heart balloons and flowers by the bed. "Big sigh, Demarco," I whisper.

My body aches, especially when I breathe. If I yawn or cough, it feels like a knife is slicing through me. I reach for the nurse's button and push it.

A minute later, a petite black-haired nurse comes in, all smiles. "Well, there you are," she says. "I'm Felicia. How are you doing? Ready for some pain meds? Let's make your Valentine's night a little happier, shall we?"

"Yes, please." It hurts so much I feel like crying.

She pushes a button that raises the head of my bed.

"Sorry I can't just set up a morphine drip. Your parents said they didn't want you to get addicted." She smiles when I groan in embarrassment. "The pills take a little longer to kick in, but you'll feel better soon."

"What's wrong with me?" I swallow the pills she hands me.

"Oh, let's see here." She checks the chart. "Your left arm is fractured, you have two cracked ribs, and we had to do some surgery for internal injuries. Looks like you are now without a spleen, and everything else got stitched up inside." She smiles. "You have a killer black eye, and some other bruises and cuts."

"I cut my finger," I say, remembering. I bring my casted arm up so I can look at it. There are three little blue Xs across my knuckle.

The nurse grins. "Yes, that too. You're definitely going to be sore for a while."

I put my arm back down, exhausted. "Please tell me who died. Do you know?"

She smiles ruefully. "Everyone knows. It was pretty big news. The man who died was Sam Rutherford. He was the driver of the snowplow."

My eyes flutter closed, but I'm not asleep. "Shit," I whisper. "I never thought about him."

"He didn't die in the crash, though. They're saying he had a massive heart attack before he hit you. The witnesses who saw the whole thing talked to the cops. They told them what you did. You're kind of a hero, Miss Julia." Felicia smiles. "The police will be by tomorrow to talk to you if you're feeling up to it."

I'm glad I didn't cause the driver's death, but I still feel terrible about it. I nod. "I guess that's fine."

"And meanwhile, there's been a sweet, very worried young man in the waiting room since last night hoping to visit you. One of the witnesses. His name is Sawyer. Do you want to see him?"

My good eye opens wide. "He's here?"

"Yes."

Ohh, dogs. My good hand flutters to my hair, which is all matted and gross. "What do I look like?"

Felicia smiles warmly and says, "You look like a girl who just saved that guy's life."

I press my lips together and nod. "That'll do. Yeah. Send him in."

Thirty-Five

He peeks his head in the door, and it's so weird to see him in this situation, with me lying here all vulnerable like this. His dark hair is disheveled and he's wearing an Angotti's shirt, as if he came straight from work.

There's a look on his face that is so pained, I almost feel like I should offer him some meds—they're starting to kick in, numbing some of my aches.

He sees my eyes are open and he stops and just stands there, six or eight feet away, like he's feeling bad for intruding. "Hey," he says, and his voice cracks on that one syllable, and then he's bringing his hand to his eyes, and his shoulders start to shake. I watch him react, and a lump rises to my throat. I am overcome.

"Oh, hell, Jules," he says after a minute. "Oh my God." It's all he can say.

"I must look really terrible to get that reaction," I say, slurring my words. I'm starting to feel a little loopy from the drugs. "Come and sit. Aren't you supposed to be at the dance or something?"

He comes over and eases into the chair by the bed and just looks at me, all this pain in his face that won't go away.

"Hey." I reach out my right hand toward him. "Why so serious?" I tease.

He takes my hand in his, holds it to his warm cheek, and leans in and hesitates, then gently strokes the hair off my forehead.

"I just—" he says, and the words are so hard for him that I want to find my Crescent wrench and yank them out. But I stay quiet. Because the truth is, he thinks he owes me this. I understand that. And he does owe me, but not for saving his life. He owes me something else.

"I—" he starts again, and this time he continues. "I'm so sorry. Jules, I'm . . . God, I was so wrong, and I didn't believe you and I should have, and I feel so . . . so guilty about it, I feel terrible about everything. About not believing you, and about the last few years, which . . ." He sighs and shakes his head. "I'm just ashamed of the way things have been, and . . . the way I treated you."

I touch my thumb to his lips and he closes his eyes.

And then he goes on. "When they couldn't get you out at first, you almost died, and they had to use the Jaws of Life . . . and Trey was begging the paramedics not to take him away because he couldn't leave you . . . I mean, I just wanted to die too. And I can't believe I let this happen because of our stupid families."

I blink hard. Jaws of Life? I almost died? "So that was me in the second bag," I murmur.

"What?"

I try to focus on him, but I'm starting to get sleepy again. "In the final vision, there were still two body bags in the snow, but one of them went away." I close my eyes and can't open them again. "That must have been me."

Sawyer squeezes my hand and presses his lips against my fingers. "I'm sorry."

"Hey," I say. The thoughts and words I mean to say are jumbled up in my head, and none of them come out at all, and then I'm slipping away again.

The third time I wake up, I see the face I've needed to see this entire time.

"Hey, good morning, Baby Bop. All purple and green."

"That's not nice," I say, grinning sleepily. "That's a great, um . . ." I point to his neck. "What's the word?"

"Scarf?"

"No."

"Noose?"

I laugh. "Ow. No, like Fred What's-His-Name wears."

"Who?"

"You know. From *Scooby-Doo*."

He raises an eyebrow. "Oh, an *ascot*."

"That's it. Is it new? Oh, hell, this joke isn't even funny anymore."

He adjusts the white brace around his neck. "You like it? It came free with the whiplash and approximately two trillion dollars in hospital costs. My sister's a crazy driver."

"It's lovely."

Trey smiles and reaches toward me, fixes my pillows. "You okay, kiddo?"

I nod. "They call me the girl who lived."

He smiles, and then grows serious. "I'm sorry I doubted you."

I take his hand. "You didn't doubt me. You believed me. Or else you wouldn't have come."

"Actually," he says, cocking his head, "I was just delivering a pizza down the street and saw the truck, thought I'd say hi."

I roll my eyes. "So, what's everybody saying? Where's Mom and Dad?"

"Mom and Dad were here overnight. You slept the whole time, they said. They just left when I came. Rowan's home getting ready for the big day-after-Valentine's rush."

I laugh and pain sears through my side again. "Stop hurting me."

"And the news story was interesting but fleeting. You had your fifteen minutes while under the knife, sad to say. But we were superheroes there for a minute or two." He leans toward me conspiratorially. "*You* were, actually. But I was happy to take credit during your incapacitation."

"Oh, good job, vice president of awesome. So . . . what do Mom and Dad think about me stealing the food truck?"

"It was a bit of a shock. They didn't know you'd ever driven it before, so obviously they think you're going to become a crazed food truck thief. And probably a mobster, too. An addicted one." He gives me a sad, sideways grin. "Truth is, they think this is all Sawyer's fault, and he's turning you into some lovesick emo rule-breaker. I'm not sure this whole thing did your relationship any favors."

I let that sink in. "Oh. That's bad." I don't yet know how I'm going to explain the truck. Or the relationship. I ponder it for a moment, and then put it aside for when I can think more clearly. "Did you talk to the police?"

"Yeah. They wanted to know if the gas line shutoff was related to our adventure, because Grand Poohbah Angotti was apparently grumbling about it. I said I knew nothing of it."

"Are you serious?" I shake my head. "He was grumbling about it? We saved his fucking restaurant and his family, and he's mad because he probably had to throw out a few pizzas? Besides, I don't remember any gas meter being turned off."

Trey regards me. "You don't?"

I grin so he knows I'm teasing. "All I know is that we saw a snowplow driving crazily, and we acted on instinct when we saw it was aiming toward our rival's restaurant. We headed it off so it wouldn't hit people, because we are human beings like that. That's it, that's all. End of story."

"So you're not going to mention the vision thing?"

"What vision thing?" I smile sweetly.

Trey laughs. "You don't know how relieved that makes me. It's gone, then?"

I nod. "It's gone."

"Phew."

"Right? Totally gone. But back to the reporters. They said what about me, exactly?" I bat my eyelashes. My lids feel all puffy and weird.

"They said a sixteen-year-old girl driving illegally with her stunningly handsome brother—who is eighteen and available, by the way—saved the world with their giant balls. Ah-ha-ha-ha."

I roll my eyes.

"They interviewed Sawyer's parents, who actually sounded grateful, and his cousin, Kate, I think her name was, who saw the whole thing from the time we were rolling. She said if we hadn't been there, the snowplow would have hit right where the dining room window is, right next to the kitchen. The cops said that with the gas meter and kitchen ovens going full blast, there could have been a tremendous explosion. But PawPaw Angotti said the gas had been manually shut off just minutes before, ruining some food—yes, he really did mention that on TV, making him look like a total douche."

"Hmm. Must have been an angel or something who turned off that gas."

"One of the world's unexplained mysteries, right alongside the Loch Ness Monster and the purpose of 'being all gangsta.'" He leans back in his chair. "Oh, and then a honey of a boy came on the interview, almost forgot. The heir to the emporium, as it were."

"Sawyer?"

"Indubitably. After his little statement, I think I'm sort of back in love with him again."

"You jerk. Tell me what he said!"

He pauses. "Okay. In all seriousness, he said something like Julia Demarco was a real hero, putting herself in harm's way to save the lives of diners and employees of a rival business, and that the Angottis were indebted to her and the entire Demarco family. And then he choked up on camera, which was superhot, and all of Chicagoland melted just a little bit that day."

"Shut up."

"True story. I'm not kidding. I watched it ad nauseam from the chair in the living room Friday night and all day yesterday."

"Did you record it?"

"Rowan recorded it just for you."

I grin. "Aww. She's so awesome."

"Ahem."

"I mean, you guys are so awesome. Thank you for coming out to find me, Trey. I'm not sure we would have made it if it hadn't been for you."

"Of course."

It's quiet for a moment. And then I tell him, "Sawyer came by. I guess it was last night. I'm kind of groggy on what day it is."

"Don't tell Mom and Dad I told you, but he's been here the entire time, almost. He's in the waiting room. He sleeps there, leaves for an hour now and then to eat or shower or whatever. Then he comes back."

My stomach flips. "Are you serious?"

"And please don't mention to Mom and Dad that you let him in here. They don't want you to have anything to do with him—they're being really cold assholes to him, actually. Dad, mostly. I mean, obviously they're upset about all of this, but I think it's also the family rivalry thing."

I close my eyes and sigh. "So this didn't cure anything."

"I don't know. Maybe it will eventually."

"Why does he come here?"

Trey snorts. "Duh. He's into you. I talked to him. He feels guilty, definitely, but he's always had a thing for you, I think. He told me he was sorry about fifty times. I asked him to make it up to me, but he rejected every one of my suggestions."

My eyes fly open. "Stay away from him, he's mine." I narrow my gaze and frown. "You really think he's into me?"

"Sister, trust me. He's into you."

"Well, why the hell has he been blowing me off since seventh grade, then?"

Trey wrinkles up his nose. "You should probably ask him yourself, but I think something strange is going on over at the Angottis that nobody knows about."

"You mean like maybe his dad is a hoarder with depression issues?"

He laughs. "Maybe. Though that would be a really weird coincidence."

I think for a moment of the conversation I had with my mother before the crash. "Mom said I wasn't the first person who had to say good-bye to an Angotti."

Trey sits up. "Say whaaa?"

"She said that. Really! And I said, 'You mean you?' And she said it wasn't her. So who does that leave, besides Dad?"

Trey sinks back down. "Well, there's me."

"You?"

"No, it wasn't me, but I don't like to be ruled out without a scandalous discussion first."

I laugh again and grab my side. "Oh, my aching— stop that!"

"I guess we have a mystery to figure out."

I nod and lie back, exhausted from the conversation, but not sleepy for once. "Two mysteries, even."

He nods and squeezes my hand. "Mom and Dad and Rowan will be back later. They're closing up early tonight to see you. Eight o'clock. So it's just you and me, and whoever might be out there, and I have homework I can do . . . just so you know."

I nod, and we share a look that says, *Bring the hot boy to Jules.*

Thirty-Six

"We need to talk about some things," I say to Sawyer as he sits down.

He nods. "We do." His dark hair hangs in little ringlets on his forehead, and he appears freshly washed today, which is better than what I can say for me. He's not wearing an Angotti's shirt anymore, either.

"First, I don't want you to mope around feeling guilty anymore, okay?"

"Okay."

"Second, what the hell happened in seventh grade that made you hate me?"

He holds my gaze, unwavering, his green eyes sending lasers into mine. "Fair question," he says finally. He drops his gaze to my bedside table and picks up a pen, weaving it through his fingers.

"You don't want to answer it?"

"No. But I need to. I'm thinking."

I take in a quick breath, moved by his honesty, ignoring the searing pain that the motion leaves behind. And I stay quiet.

"Where to start," he says, lost in thought. "My grandfather," he says eventually, "is a very controlling man."

I nod.

"He used to hit me."

My eyes spring open wide. "Your *grand*father? Didn't your parents stop him?"

He hesitates. "No. They didn't. My mother couldn't, and my father was angry enough that he wouldn't."

"I don't get it. Why couldn't your mother stop him? What kind of a—"

He sets the pen down and clasps his hands together, staring down at them. I look at his hands too and remember the feel of his touch on my cheek. And then he looks up at me again, his eyes unwavering for an almost frightening amount of time.

"Your father and my mother had an affair, Jules."

The words take a moment to register. "What?" I say, incredulous.

"My mother just told me everything yesterday, after all

of this—" He waves his hand at me, at the hospital. "When I was so angry and upset, and I didn't understand why things had to be the way they are between us. She made me promise not to tell you, but I can't help it. I think you need to know."

I bring my hand to my hair and try to work my fingers through it. It's weird. I don't feel anything about this. No emotion, nothing. And then I think about my poor mother, and my heart cracks. "When?" I say.

"A long time ago, when we were really young."

"Wow." I stare up at the ceiling, trying to process it.

"It was short, and Mom said both of them eventually realized it was a mistake, but it happened," Sawyer says. "I can't believe she told me all of this, but she'd been drinking. It was late." He glances at the door and then says quietly, "She said they planned to leave their spouses, combine restaurant assets, and become an enterprise. Take over business from the chains, sell products commercially and all that."

My mouth drops open. "Products? Made from secret family recipes?"

"Yes." Sawyer takes a deep breath and can't look at me. "From what I know, your father gave my mother his family's special sauce recipe, which my grandfather had been after for years. When your dad and my mom broke it off, and my father and grandfather found out, they were seriously pissed off. To try to redeem herself, my mother gave them the recipe. Kind of a last-ditch effort to try to diffuse things and keep the family together." He stares at the ground. "And my grandfather took it. And he patented it."

"You are not serious." I look at him in wonder. "That's probably what put my grandfather into his big downward spiral. Betrayed by his son and his biggest rival." A new realization hits me. "Maybe that's my dad's problem. It's the guilt. Not just losing the recipe, but driving his father to kill himself. Holy shit."

Sawyer nods. "It all sounds extremely dramatic, but that's because it was, according to my mom."

"Yes."

Sawyer looks up at me, remorseful. "When you and I were in first grade, our stolen sauce line went to market, and it was a hit. Your father tried to sue us, but he didn't have the proof he needed to win. It was a verbal recipe, handed down for generations, my mom said. He'd known it by heart. Never wrote it down."

"Oh my God," I say. "That's when the hoarding started." All the recipes and cookbooks piled up in our apartment. None of them holding a candle to the one that remained unwritten.

Sawyer doesn't say anything for a minute, and I stare at the ceiling, letting everything sink in.

"My grandfather was furious that your dad would dare

to sue him. My father was hurt and angry over my mother messing around. And your parents had plenty of reason to hate us as well. So when you and I ended up becoming friends, it practically started a war all over again."

"Wow," is all I can say. I struggle to sit up, and Sawyer rises to help me. He lifts me gently, and his fingers linger on my shoulders before he sits back down.

"We hid our friendship really well, for a while, at least," he says ruefully. "Didn't we?"

"Until I saw you—" I say as he says, "Until the day before—"

"Seventh grade," we say together.

"My father saw you with your dad, saw your smile, and he watched my face light up to see you. He knew it wasn't just an acquaintance kind of smile. Back at home we 'had a talk,' which consisted of him and my grandfather telling me I was not to speak to you again, ever. When I protested, my grandfather got so enraged, he grabbed me by the collar and dragged me to my room. And then he started hitting me."

"Oh, Sawyer," I whisper.

He shoves his chair back and starts working his hands together. "He beat me pretty hard, but not anywhere you could see bruises. He was very careful about that. My mother couldn't do anything—he threatened her, too, threatened to force my dad to divorce her after what she'd done, take us kids away from her, and leave her with no money."

"That's insane."

"It's different when a man like that lives with you. Holds so much power over you—there's no way you could understand." He taps his fingers on the chair arms, distraught. "So I agreed to stop talking to you just to get him to lay off me. And that time," he says, standing up and starting to pace around the bed, "that one time you and I had to do a project together, he found out somehow. And he beat me up, even though I cried and told him that I didn't have any control over who got paired up. It didn't matter. He wanted to make sure we never spent time together, ever again."

I don't know what to say.

Sawyer paces, agitated. "But the worst thing is that I let him hold that over me so long, even up until last week, even though I could probably take him in a fight now if I had to. He just kept that fear and control over me like he has over my parents, and I was just dead inside. All that time I didn't talk to you, Jules, I wanted to. I watched you. I saw your hurt face and I made a choice against you. I didn't do the right thing." He rips his fingers through his hair and I can tell he's upset at himself. "I'm so beyond sorry. And I'm not letting that happen ever again, even if it means I have to walk out on all of them."

He comes over to the bed and grips the side rail. "I can't believe I kept walking away from you instead of them, over and over. Even after you said . . . what you said . . . in the middle of the night. And the other day at school. It killed me, walking away from you at lunch, but . . ." He shakes his head. "It's no excuse. But then you almost died because you wanted to save me. And it finally sank in. I'm the biggest idiot on the planet. And I'm done making bad choices out of fear."

I don't have any words to say. All I can do is watch him pull his heart out and set it in front of me. Watch him tell me he cared about me too, all that time. Watch him say how sorry he is, how much he wants to be the opposite of the kind of guy that his grandfather and father are. Watch him stand there, asking me to give him another chance.

And what am I supposed to do?

Thirty-Seven

But before I can say anything to Sawyer, strangers wearing scrubs come in to announce the removal of my catheter. Awesome. Thanks, guys.

Sawyer makes a hasty retreat, and before you know it, I have my faculties back, and they have me easing out of bed and standing, and then walking a few steps, and every muscle in my entire body screams at me. By the time I get back in bed and have some dinner, I'm done for. Trey comes back to say good night, and he looks tired too.

And as much as I want to continue the conversation with Sawyer, I definitely need to rest. I tell Trey to send Sawyer home. With Mom and Dad coming, there's no reason for him to stay and make the situation worse.

I'm not really sure what to think about what Sawyer

told me, and it's a little hard to process. Maybe because it's so weird to imagine my dad having an affair, and maybe because of the painkillers—everything is taking just a little longer to comprehend these days. But what I have comprehended is that my dad is a big rotten cheater, and my mom just keeps smiling that agonized smile all the time, and now I think I know why. Just who the hell does he think he is?

I don't want to see Dad, that's for sure. Before Sawyer left, I promised him I wouldn't say anything. I don't want to cause more problems between our families, especially now.

When my parents come they wake me up, and I remember all over again.

It's like I'm looking at two strangers. I wonder why my mom stayed with him. I wonder why Mr. Angotti stayed with Sawyer's mom. Maybe it was for our sakes.

I can't actually stand the thought of talking to my father right now, so I just focus on Mom and Rowan. They made it through Valentine's Day without Trey or me, and customers were sympathetic. Today, too, the place was packed with supporters, they said. Seems we got an unexpected sympathy rush out of the ordeal, which is awesome. I guess. Dad hired Aunt Mary's deadbeat son, our cousin Nick, to help out for a while until Trey is feeling up to coming back.

And then there's Rowan. Poor girl. She never gets a break. I think of all the times she's covered for me lately, and she doesn't complain. I try to make her feel awesome. I wish Mom and Dad would go away for a while so I can just talk to her. Find out how her boyfriend is. See how she's doing with everything.

Before they go home, my father, who's been agitating over in the corner all alone, apparently feels like he just has to say something.

"Now that you're feeling a little better," he says, "I want to make sure you only let family in to see you. Nobody else. Okay? And soon you'll be home."

I see my mother flash him an annoyed look, and Rowan's eyes go wide. I think about fighting him on it because it's stupid, but I'm also really tired and ready to sleep. "Who else is there besides family?" I say. "Of course, Dad. I don't want anybody else seeing me like this."

"And then we'll talk about why you would steal the food truck just to go see that hooligan."

I nod. "Fine."

He hesitates, then seems satisfied. I yawn, trying not to split my chest in half. "I'm really tired, guys," I say. "They're talking about sending me home Tuesday. I just want to get there. So I'm going to sleep now, okay? Please don't stay. You need your rest too. I'll sleep like a baby with these meds. I'm fine, okay?"

"Of course," Mom says, and she stands up. I'm a little surprised she doesn't argue, but she seems preoccupied. "Come on, Antonio," she says to Dad. "We'll see you tomorrow, sweetheart." Her effervescent smile is as fake as they come.

In the morning, my task is to take a shower, and I actually see for the first time all the places I have cuts and contusions. My entire outer left thigh and butt cheek are so purple they're almost black from the door smashing in on me. They said it was amazing I didn't break my hip or leg. I've got stitches in my scalp, my chin, and one knee in addition to my stomach from surgery and my knuckle from the Crescent wrench. My black eye is less puffy but still purple with a hint of yellow.

After the shower a volunteer comes in and does my hair and makeup, which almost makes me cry because it's so sweet. It feels good to not look like a total train wreck again. When I think of how I looked in the hospital bed, I know that Sawyer could have run away screaming, but he must really like me if he could stand to look at me that way. I feel a little extra energy today coming from inside— relief, or happiness, I guess.

Once I'm all fresh and clean, my next required task is to take a walk down the hallway. The day is full of challenges, isn't it? Mom stops by before the restaurant opens to bring me one of her homemade bran muffins, which are amazingly delicious. She must have gotten up early to make them, and once again I feel a pain in my chest for her. She sits for a bit, and we just talk about our days, and avoid talking about anything that could get weird.

But ever since Mom told me that I wasn't the first to have to say good-bye to an Angotti, I sense she wants to talk about something more. And for the first time, I actually think that's a good idea. Maybe it's because of what Sawyer told me about my father, so I feel sorry for her now or something. But maybe because I think she knows that I'm really in love with Sawyer, and she's okay with it. It wouldn't be a bad thing to have her on my side.

But that talk doesn't happen.

When she leaves, I have lunch and a nap, just killing time waiting and hoping for visitors after school. Hoping Sawyer comes back.

I wonder idly what happened to my cell phone in this whole ordeal. All I know is that I don't have it. It's probably smashed to bits.

Trey and Rowan come straight from school. "Trey's a freaking hero," Rowan says as they burst into the room. "Everybody loves him. He won't stop talking about his own awesomeness." She flops into the chair next to my bed, and I can hardly contain my delight. I missed my sibs.

No matter how crowded the house can be, it's still fun to be crowded with them.

"I'm not surprised," I say. "He can't ever get enough attention."

"Hi. I'm right here," he says.

"See?" says Rowan. "As if seeing him isn't enough, he has to announce his presence."

"It's disgusting," I say.

Trey's jaw drops. "Fine," he says. "I'll just go hang out with my new BFF, Sawyer Angotti."

"What??" both Rowan and I exclaim.

"We had lunch today in the caf," Trey says.

"I hate you."

"Me too!" Rowan says, and then turns to me. "Wait, why do we hate him?"

"Because we're jealous, dumbhead."

"I'm not jealous. I don't get what you two see in him. He's so . . . broody and dark and Italian."

Trey thinks for a moment and says, "You know, Rowan's right. I could go for a nice Scandinavian."

Rowan agrees with a hearty nod and a secret smile at me. "Blonds are hot."

"You know who's hot?" Trey asks. "Jules Demarco. Amazing what a shower does for that girl."

I sink back into my pillows with a grin, feeling like all is well in the world.

•   •   •

When they leave to get to the restaurant before the rush, there's a knock at the door, and I know it's him. I can feel it. "Come in," I say.

He pushes open the door and ducks his head in a shy sort of way, which makes my thighs ache, and not because of the bruises. He's holding a bunch of grocery store flowers with the price sticker still on them. He hands them to me awkwardly. "I'm sort of new at this," he says. "The clerk at Jewel said you'd definitely like these."

I squelch a grin. "You asked for help?"

"Sure," he said. "My cousin Kate said I should bring you flowers, which—I know, I know—I didn't need her to tell me that, thank you very much. But I didn't really know, like, what kind."

"I love them," I say, and I can't stop grinning.

And then, from his shirt pocket, he pulls something else out and hands it to me. "Do you still like these?" It's a butterscotch sucker from their candy jar.

I stare at it, take it in my hand. "Yeah," I say. "I do." Okay . . . that almost made me cry. And I know that there's no question that I will give him a chance to do things differently, to stand up for the things he really wants.

I love you, I want to say. But it feels very weird today to say something like that. Now that the danger is over, that is, and it appears we'll both live. At least until our parents find out we're hanging out again, anyway.

I slip my hand in his like it's the most natural thing in the world, and we're talking like we're sixth graders again, sitting under the slide with our suckers and doing that innocent, flirty thing. Every time he says something funny, I laugh even though it hurts, and when he blinks those long lashes and looks at me with that shy grin, my stomach flips. He stays for hours, and I want the night to go on forever.

Sadly, we lose track of time.

Thirty-Eight

When my parents come in and see that Angotti boy holding my hand, and they see the flowers in the crook of my broken arm, I think my father is going to have an aneurysm. Sawyer stands up faster than the speed of light and his chair topples to the floor behind him.

I struggle to sit up.

"Get out," my father says to Sawyer.

Sawyer looks fleetingly to me, then back to my father. "Sir," he says, and I feel a rush of warmth when he doesn't just go. "Can we talk about this?"

"No. Out." My father points to the door. He's being calm. Too calm. "You are not to see my daughter again."

"Mr. Demarco," he says, "Trey and Jules saved our restaurant and our lives, and I'm just—"

"Well, maybe they shouldn't have done that. Did you look at her? She almost *died* because of you!"

"I know, sir, and we are very grate—"

"If you don't get out of this room right now, I will call security."

I can hardly breathe. "Dad, stop!" I say. "Don't be crazy." I cringe after I say it. "He's on his way out anyway, and I'm glad he stopped by, and I hope our families—"

"Pipe dreams!" my father says bitterly. "Our families will never be friendly as long as I'm alive, and you, young lady, had better get that figured out right now. This is over. Do you both hear me?"

Sawyer stands his ground and stays cool, and in that moment, I see him acting on his own desire to be different from the father and grandfather he described yesterday. "I'm sorry you feel that way, sir," he says in a calm voice, yet he commands the room. "I'll leave now out of respect for you. But I'll never leave Jules again because of something personal that happened between other people, so you might want to get used to seeing me around." He gives me a look that makes my heart quake, and then he smiles politely at my mother. "Thank you for what your family did for my family, Mrs. Demarco," he says. And then he slips out.

My father slams the door behind him.

"Antonio!" my mother says, her voice raised, which is exceedingly rare.

He startles and looks at her. "What?"

She shakes her head. "Act your age once, will you? Honestly. We're in a hospital, for Christ's sake." I've never heard her talk like that before. Ever. "Maybe you should go cool off so I don't call security on *you*."

"Why, what did I do?"

"That boy did nothing to you. Leave him alone."

"He is just as his family is," Dad says.

"Oh my dogs," I say, disgusted. "You don't know anything about him! And if he is as his family is, then what does that make me? Am I just as my family is too? A bitter, psychopathic hoarder?"

I don't know if it was the drugs. I think it probably was—I'm pretty good at hiding my thoughts otherwise. At least I didn't call him a cheater. I don't think I did, anyway. Everything got a little fuzzy right around then.

Mom says a hasty good-bye before he can explode, and she drags him out of the room.

By the time I get discharged on Tuesday, my father and I haven't spoken one word to each other, and it looks like we won't be speaking anytime soon. And frankly, I'm really fine with that, because he's acting like the biggest asshole on the planet.

I spend the next week and a half at home and I can't stand it. No cell phone, no communication with Sawyer other than a few e-mails. My father has the home phone forwarded to the restaurant so that I can't receive any calls, and he threatens to watch the phone bill like a hawk to see if I'm calling anybody. I argue and fight, and it only makes things worse—he takes the Internet cable with him to the restaurant whenever I'm home alone. Stupidly, I talked him right out of getting me a replacement cell phone . . . at least until I'm out of this prison and I need one for deliveries again.

In the evenings up in our room Rowan entertains me with a few tidbits about her video chats with Charlie, whose full name is Charles Broderick Banks, and who isn't really homeschooled—he has a tutor and a house in the Hamptons and has never made a pizza in his life. Rowan's going to keep her secret from Mom and Dad for a while longer. Hopefully they'll calm down enough to be reasonable about it, but I have a feeling Rowan won't be going to New York anytime soon. And that's really sad, because Charlie seems like a good guy.

And thank dog for Trey, who is acting as a secret liaison between Sawyer and me. I honestly don't know what I'd do without him right now. On the last Friday of my confinement, Trey comes home with a note for me in a sealed envelope. When I am alone, I open it, and in Sawyer's old familiar handwriting, I read:

*I don't want to risk you getting caught,
but I really have to see you as soon
as possible. I'll be by your back door
tonight at 2 a.m. If you can't come
down, I understand.*

Miss you so much. Want to hold you . . .

SA

I die a little.
No, a lot.

I take a nap in the late afternoon to prepare, and wait
impatiently for everyone to come back up to the apartment and go to bed. I fake sleeping, and finally everyone
else is sleeping too. I hope.

At 1:45 a.m. I slip out of bed and put my clothes on.
I'm starting to get the hang of dressing with my cast on my
arm, but it still takes me a while. I peek out my bedroom
window, and there's a car out there with no fresh snow on
it. I think it's his car. I ease my way out of the bedroom,
careful not to make any noise with doors, grab my coat,
and sneak down the stairs, taking each step gingerly. All I
know is that if I get caught, I sure as hell can't run very
fast right now.

When I open the door, a figure gets out of the car and closes the door softly, and then he lopes over a snowdrift and comes to me. I bite my lip and close the door behind me.

The grin I expect isn't there, only an anxious, hungry look. He reaches for me, slips his fingers gently into my hair, and looks at me like I'm water and he's the desert. Gently he pushes me back a step so I can lean against the wall, and then, without a word, he traces his finger over my lips and I'm mesmerized. He leans in and his lips brush mine, and I'm surprised and thrilled and trying to make sure I'll never forget my first kiss, but soon he's pressing harder and I'm reaching for him and I can't be bothered to think or remember anything at all. I just need to be in it and try to breathe without hurting anything.

I slide my arm inside his jacket and run my hand around his waist, feeling the warmth of his back and holding him like he's the first human I've ever touched before. As we learn how to kiss, I feel him touching me, caressing my hair, being careful around my sore spots, and I never want him to let go.

When our lips part and his tongue finds mine, we are warm and breathing hard into the cold February night. And when we stop for air, I think about all we've been through with the vision and the crash, and nine years of family rivalry. I feel like if I can overcome that, I can overcome anything. And while it won't be fun to fight my dad, I will do what is necessary to allow myself to have this moment again, and soon. I won't let him take this from me. Not now. Not ever again. As long as Sawyer is with me, we can do this.

I look up at him, touch his cheek. "Hey," I say softly, my voice stuck somewhere south of my throat. "That was totally worth a trip down the stairs."

But he doesn't smile. He just looks at me with this fear in his eyes, and my heart drops into my gut. "What's wrong?" I whisper.

He opens his mouth to say something, and then closes it again. "Jules," he says, like it's agony to say it. It's all he can say.

I stand up straight, grip his jacket. "What's going on?" And then I suck in a breath. "Is this a good-bye? Sawyer, say something. Don't scare me."

He shifts his glance away to the side, biting his lip, and then he takes a step back and his hand finds mine. He turns, and with his other hand he points toward Chicago, far off in the distance. "You know that billboard?" he says, his voice a shaky mess.

I grip his hand and fall back against the wall as the question bounces around in my head. Pain sears through me. I can't breathe. "What? What did you say?"

He swallows hard. I can see his Adam's apple bob in

the light of the neon Demarco's sign. "That billboard. Jose Cuervo," he says, his voice dull.

I can't breathe. "Yes."

He turns to look at me. "There's something else on it now."

"Oh, God. No." I grip his arm and murmur what I know has to be true. "And only you can see it."

He nods slowly and, in a whisper, echoes my words. "Only I can see it."

We hold each other, staring off toward a billboard that displays a hint of the future only Sawyer can see. And as we stand there, thinking about the incredible heartache of the visions and the burden of it all, I hear the heavy footfalls of a bitter, pissed-off man coming down the stairwell of my home. I grip Sawyer's arm tighter in front of me, ready to stand my ground or run if I have to, and all I can think about is that this crazy drama in our messed-up lives isn't even close to being over. And before it ends, one or both of us could wind up in a body bag.

Again.